Easter 1982

To Mum
With love
Elaine

D0457099

By STRATIS HAVIARAS

POETRY
Η Κυρια με την Πυξιδα
  The Lady with a Compass (1963)*
Βερολινο
  Berlin (1965)*
Η Νυχτα του Ξυλοποδαρου
  The Night of the Stiltwalker (1967)*
Νεκροφανεια
  Apparent Death (1972)*

Crossing the River Twice (1976)

FICTION
When the Tree Sings (1979)

EDITOR
35 Post-War Greek Poets (1972)
The Poet's Voice (1978)

Published only in Greek

When the Tree Sings

STRATIS HAVIARAS

Drawings by Fred Marcellino

Simon and Schuster • New York

Copyright © 1979 by Stratis Haviaras
All rights reserved
including the right of reproduction
in whole or in part in any form
Published by Simon and Schuster
A Division of Gulf & Western Corporation
Simon & Schuster Building
Rockefeller Center
1230 Avenue of the Americas
New York, New York 10020

Designed by Eve Metz
Manufactured in the United States of America

2 3 4 5 6 7 8 9 10

Library of Congress Cataloging in Publication Data

Haviaras, Stratis, date.
    When the tree sings.

    I. Title.
PZ4.H3853Wh   [PS3558.A783]   813'.5'4   78-27684

ISBN 0-671-24754-9

FOR HEATHER ELLEN

The Lacedaemonians announced that the Helots were to choose from their ranks those who had distinguished themselves in the war, so that these might be given their liberty. About 2000 of them were selected who went wreathed to the temples as though they were already free. But shortly afterward the Lacedaemonians cut them all down, in secret.
    —Thucydides, Book IV, LXXX

Prologue

This land, a narrow strip between rocks and seas, can afford only so many of us. It has no trees, no water—only an illusion of trees and water. The old springs are choked, desecrated with corpses of animals and men. We dig new wells for water, but do not find it. Old Tryfos, who knows how to pin down a vein, walks over, and, putting an ear to the ground, he listens carefully. He snaps a green twig, carrying it around to see if its tip will bend earthward, but it does not; to see if its fine leaves will quiver and turn downward, but they don't. The old expert understands the tyranny and doesn't get discouraged. "Maybe here," he says, "maybe there." He keeps on until the twig wilts, and when it wilts he picks a fresh one. He puts his ear down to listen again, and if he thinks he hears something, he smells the earth; he puts a bit of dirt in his mouth to taste it, saying, "Maybe here," but he's almost convinced there is nothing—dog piss perhaps, or a man buried, decomposing. He marks the earth and cuts another twig. Each time a leaf turns its cheek, he marks the earth again: Maybe here. He gets his pay in kind, he takes his leave, and the next morning we cross ourselves and start digging. Each time

9

the pickaxe strikes the ground, the rock responds with a sheaf of sparks. Before the water vein come the veins of the rock: thin veins, veins filled with clay. We drive a wedge and the rock sighs; we drive another and the rock coughs. When a whole big chunk comes off, it's a great occasion. We smell the underside of the stone, we lick it—we shake our heads, we go on digging. Four, five, seven strides deep and still no water. We cover half of the mouth of the well, hoping to collect some rain water in it. It doesn't rain that often, and when it does it washes off the mountainside, rushing down to the sea. We fix a grille and a screen at the mouth of the well to keep the dead animals out, but the water still smells, still tastes funny; we won't drink from it, yet we keep saying, "It's good for washing clothes; it's great for washing your hair. It really cleans your hair well and makes it silky."

I

I was sitting on the front steps of an abandoned house, waiting. Someone had lit a small fire to keep me warm after the sun went down. The flames were keeping the stray dogs at bay. I did not know how close to the fire I should be. I was hot and cold at the same time. I had to wait. When the dogs came closer, sniffing and growling, I saw myself rising from the steps, then holding still in mid-air. I felt good. I was fascinated by the fire as it went out, slowly. When the dogs left, I stretched my arms and legs downward, trying to fall. Nothing happened. I expected someone to call my name. I spent some time watching the stars get dizzy. An old man came by, holding a guitar in his arms. He started a new fire. He began to nod. Then one of the dogs came back and curled up next to him. The old man stretched out his hand and stroked the dog's head without looking at it. The dog did not bite him. I was warm again. I felt good. Late at night, the old man played his guitar, and I began to move my arms and legs, and to nod like him, but he didn't look at me. He never saw me, and he never called my name.

Then another man came along, saying that my

mother had another child. "But don't worry, she hasn't given up hope of your returning someday."

How did he know my mother?

"My name is Phlox," he said. "I am a puppeteer. . . . I make things up."

Funny man. He threw some more wood on the fire, smiling. "I have to go now," he added.

The old man was playing his guitar more and more loudly. He was angry.

The smoke was getting in my eyes. I rubbed them until I saw two widening rings of bright water.

"That's good," said Phlox. "That will help you sleep and grow up." Then I heard his voice again from a distance: "Grow down, grow down, is what I mean."

It took me a long time to accustom myself to his sense of humor. I closed my eyes, went to sleep, and dreamed that I was falling. It was a breathtaking fall, and I was sure neither Phlox nor the old man was there any longer to catch me.

That's how children were sorted out in our town: some of them ended up in the fire, or were finished off by the dogs.

WATER   I looked into the water and saw my face, and the circles around it widening, then returning diminished.

"Kiss the water before drinking it, or you'll lose it," said Phlox. And he said, "When there's no water to drink there's nothing of anything, and you're alone in the world, and unfinished."

"That's not water," argued the old man without looking at Phlox; "that's a shadow. . . . Ah, this little bird drinks only by looking upward, catching the raindrops as they fall."

I looked into the water and saw the trinity of the clover, and the clouds breaking up with small bursts. There were no stars in the sky.

"There's plenty of stars," argued the old man.

"When you're blind, you can see things without looking at them," whispered Phlox so the old man wouldn't hear.

"And only when you're hard of hearing can you really listen," added the old man.

There was lightning in the east, thunder in the west, and driving rain from the south. I didn't look up. I marveled at a single raindrop on a leaf, then at the leaf itself.

"Look, you're missing the rain," shouted Phlox.

The spine of that leaf was about to bend under the weight of that drop. It bent. I didn't miss the rain. Lower down there was another drop.

"That one's caught in a web," said Phlox.

I considered the spider. She moved toward that drop with caution. Her caution seemed to be part of a ritual: she just wouldn't drink that raindrop before wrapping it up in silk.

I did not miss the rain. Like the rain, the spider devised a string of silk which she climbed down safely, although the upper end of her string was tied to nothing.

When the sun came out, the little bird was still looking upward, stunned, with a red poppy unfolding slowly in its cracked beak.

When the sun came out, delicate morning glories made music too, and sang with a thousand mouths. And the big clay jar in front of the ruined house was full of different voices.

"Words for the winter," said Phlox, "your mother's voice and your father's voice."

He glanced at me as if he expected a question. He looked worried. I didn't ask the question, and he didn't answer it. He was embarrassed.

"I wish I knew," he sighed.

THE SHADOW SCREEN

At home Phlox was always busy making puppets, or thinking up stories for his shadow theater. Phlox played only on Sunday evenings. His screen was a stretched bedsheet. He'd pin a perforated paper house on it, light a kerosene lamp, clear his throat: "Good evening ladies and lords . . ." Blackeye was the foremost character. There were others: Block-head. Grammarian. Thug. Alexander the Great. Mermaid & Co. Heroes and tyrants, jokers, troub-lemakers. A lovely princess with long blond braids down to her ass. Another with breasts big enough to feed a dozen children.

"How come little children float in the air like that?"

"They are hungry. When all they swallow is air, they rise like balloons, and they won't come down unless somebody feeds them, or pops them with a pin."

For many months, Phlox and I shared that same ruined house. To forget our hunger, we often went behind the screen, trying out puppets and episodes for a new play. Sometimes Phlox moved the wrong characters across the screen, or put the wrong words in their mouths, naming heroes after their defeated enemies, and the tyrants seemed to live forever.

"But why?"

"So we can have new heroes all the time. Here, let's have another one right now."

Phlox drew one on a sheet of cardboard. The

puppet looked like me, a bit older. He named it Teo.

"Now it's your turn."

I took the pencil and started from the top of the forehead down, the nose crooked, the lips parted in a perpetual smile. Another line all the way to the chin and to the lower part of the throat. Top of the forehead again, the hair short, straight, but like a whirlwind at the top of the head, half a circle, and down the vertical nerve of the nape. An eye then, which is hard to capture in profile, a single nostril then, and an ear that looks like a conch. Here's the body. Here's an arm, and the second arm's easy. Here's a leg, and it looks fine; make it two.

"That's me, all right," said Phlox. "Now divide the body at the waist for agility, and make the legs a little thinner so he can run fast."

"Why?"

"He looks suspicious, dangerous. Pretty soon the authorities will be after him."

Phlox showed me how to cut the outline of my drawing limb by limb with a pair of scissors, and, using a screwdriver, we punched holes so the puppet's features could show through on the screen; then we punched what Phlox called structural holes. We assembled the parts, linking them with seven knots, then glued transparent yellow, green, and red paper over the holes. Phlox moved the lamp behind the screen, and the puppets we had named after ourselves walked right in and shook hands, praising each other's looks.

"Pretty soon you'll be on your own," said Phlox.

We shook hands.

". . . On the other hand, you might be too young to be on your own. Maybe you should go to live with your relatives for a year or so."

"I don't remember having any relatives."

Phlox's face became worried. "You must try hard to remember," he said.

I remembered dipping my hand in a bucket of milk and licking my fingers. When the old woman killed the calf on the stone, its blood smelled as sweet as its mother's milk. My youngest cousin and I, and a neighborhood kid who had only one eye, used to play around the calf a lot that summer. When we were told to tie a red ribbon around its neck, we thought it was a great idea, but in the morning we gathered outside the barn to watch silently as the old woman passed the knife through the calf's neck. We hid behind the door, trembling, and the shadows came to lick the blood from the stone.

And I remembered watching the wind send the leaves of a singing tree eastward. The sparrows flew against the wind, then perched on the branches. High above them, the first autumn clouds and a reverberation of thunder. Under the tree the water was dark, its surface wrinkled. Then seagulls began to mix with sparrows, and the mare raised her head, neighing. The wind brought dust, and a smell of rain and sulphur. I saw the old woman come out of the hut, scraping the leftovers of the lunch from a blackened clay pot. I saw the wind lift her apron to her face. The dog approached her, wagging his tail. My cousin Philippos and the one-eyed kid, whose name was Flisvos, passed by, carrying a basketful of dark red grapes. When they reached the crossroads, they stopped and changed hands. The dog gobbled up the leftovers and had a drink of water. The old woman rinsed the pot, and for a moment she stopped and stared at the surface of the small pool between the well and the tree. That's where the first raindrop fell and leaped again into the air, only darker.

But Phlox didn't believe me. He thought I was making all this up, the way he made up his stories for the shadow theater. "This land is arid," he said.

"It has no trees, no water—only an illusion of trees and water."

Phlox knew how to say out loud all kinds of things that I often wanted to say but was unable to put into words. But a few days later, the enemy outlawed all shadow theater performances in public as subversive, and Phlox had to take his puppets and run.

II

GRAND-
MOTHER

"Grandma, why do you have to kneel in order to pray?"

"Small gods are more lovable."

"Grandma, why do your knees bleed when you kneel?"

"There was a time when stones used to be softer."

"Grandma, are you afraid of the Devil's ways?"

"Like the saints, devils were canonized by the church."

"Grandma, why don't you stare at the night sky like me?"

"Dried-up wells no longer bear stars."

I drew her picture on a sheet of cardboard, but when I had finished, she didn't look like her picture. The black scarf matched; the wrinkles matched; the toothless mouth and the single gold tooth matched; but something didn't, and I couldn't tell what it was.

"Grandma, why did your face change while I was making your picture?"

She went from room to room busily calling the cat: "Here kitty-kitty, here kitty-kitty . . ."

Grandmother never had a cat. I started another drawing without looking at her. She walked back on tiptoe and looked at it over my shoulder.

"Where's the cat?" I asked.

"What cat?" she said.

I stared into her eyes. She didn't blink. I went back to the drawing. "The cat you were calling a minute ago," I said.

"Meow," she said.

I drew the pupils of her eyes gray, pointed, sharp like a cat's, and her picture came to life.

"Meow," she said again.

Every summer before the war, the people in our town moved to the country to work in the fields. June, July, and August the houses were locked up and the roads deserted. A thick layer of dust covered the yards and the flower gardens. The plants grew thin and sickly without care and water. Heat, a dazzling light, stillness, and the day endless. The late afternoon breeze from the sea never seemed to find its way to the narrow winding streets. And people used to tell scary stories about the deserted town. Stories about the dead coming back to add to our troubles.

So in September, just before everybody moved back to town, a dozen men ran through the streets to chase the dead away with other, stranger sounds: goat bells, cymbals, tambourines, and shouts. But when they reached the square, they always stopped. They looked at each other, and as they raised their shoulders, their hands seemed empty. No one could ever get used to that square: vast, its emptiness emphasized by a broken crate on wheels, a dried-up fountain, and a statue so old that nobody remembered who had sculpted it or who the woman was who had posed for it. Some said her name was Aphrodite, the first woman to ride a bicycle in our town, the first person to die in a traffic accident. In the small city hall, there's still a picture of the square by a local artist who became famous:

SUMMER
MYSTERIES

the old yellowing buildings with domes, arches, arcades—all empty, all abandoned for the summer or forever. Next to the statue of the sleeping woman, right on the black cobblestones, one can see a bunch of artichokes, and in the distance the 1:33 P.M. locomotive puffing white smoke, ready to depart without passengers and without an engineer.

WAR   The enemy soldiers loaded the good wheat into their trucks and took it away. And then they took the horses away. The horses, the goats, and the sheep. The chickens, the ducks, and the geese. The pigs! And when the farming season was over, they took the men away. The men and, selectively, the women.

"The enemy is not all that hungry," said Grandmother. "The reason he eats a lot is to keep others from eating."

Grandmother knew a lot about the enemy, and I liked the way she spoke. I offered her a partnership in my future shadow theater company, but she turned me down, saying, "I'd rather be in the audience."

The enemy made records, destination charts, and sent the hostages away. Words that were always there, but almost never used, words that we didn't even know existed, became more than familiar: *Forced Labor, Labor Camps, Concentration Camps, Death Camps, Torture Chambers, Gas Chambers, Extermination Chambers.* Camps and Chambers.

And when winter came, we watched the sparrows scratching the ice for food and not finding it. We too were hungry. We thought of setting traps to catch the sparrows and eat them, but somehow we kept postponing it, kept forgetting about it. The language was catching up faster: *Hunger* became *Famine. Dying* was reduced to *Wiped Out Clean*, or just *Wiped*. The enemy *Enforced the Law*, and we *Sustained the Losses*. Our people began to meet in basements secretly. In many towns, men and women got together, saying, "Enough is enough," and had long discussions about what was to be done. There were arguments.

"Informers," said Grandmother. "In each group there was at least one enemy informer. But the idea of fighting took hold."

Many of our people took to the mountains, then came down to attack remote garrisons, or to derail supply trains. There were quick reprisals: for each train destroyed, or enemy soldier killed, fifty of our own people were to be shot. *Reprisals*.

"The enemy thinks he's superior," said Grandmother, "but that doesn't necessarily make us inferior."

"What's that supposed to mean, Grandmother?"

"We can be as brutal as the enemy," said Grandmother, shaking her head.

"Then how come we don't kill fifty enemy soldiers when they kill one of us?"

"Our kill has quality," she said.

Grandmother was stranger than Phlox, but she too knew how to say out loud all sorts of things that I wanted to say but was unable to put into words. My collection of shadow theater puppets was increasing steadily. Besides the stock characters, I already owned Grandmother, Flisvos and Philippos, the Commandant, and Lekas the Informer. Then I began to carry a little notebook and pencil in my pocket and to write down all kinds of thoughts and ideas that would enrich my shadow theater plays. Grandmother didn't mind my performances. Since there was no longer anything to cook in the kitchen, I stretched my screen across the opening of the pantry, and I didn't have to take it down at the end of the show.

HUNGER
TALES

I sat at the window sill and looked out. Several dark, rainy clouds passed by, quickly covering the moon, and I saw their shadows climbing up and down the houses and moving northward. Suddenly, something stirred within my brain, and I was frightened. "Hunger's a tremor," I said. "Hunger's a toothless mouth; and when it opens, a black umbrella opens within it, and the mouth can't see a thing. Hunger surrounds it, hunger surrenders it," I said. I lit the kerosene lamp behind the screen, and let my puppets loose.

An old man began to dig with teeth and nails for roots, moaning weakly from hunger.

Then two kids were blown to pieces by a land mine as they tried to disarm it and use the dynamite cakes to kill fish in the bay. I saw their little arms in smoking sleeves hung from a fig tree, trembling—so simple.

And I saw a woman in black overcome by crows, and a younger woman crawl to the roadside, dragging her entrails over the dust.

There were other stories:

Dead birds were found in wells almost daily. There was talk about a virgin giving birth to a monster, but no one's description of it matched another's. Everyone blamed the drought. When it finally rained, the water was muddy, and the Grammarian said he found small fish in the puddles—poisoned fish.

And the old ikons of the Mother of God were disappearing from the churches, and pictures of a younger Mary began to appear. She no longer had the dark crescents below her eyes, she no longer had wrinkles. Tears, yes, two sparkling tears on her rosy cheeks, but she looked happy, and the child in her arms was not dark, but white, milk-white, as if he hadn't yet been out in the sun. Nobody thought the change was a miracle, and the deacons on the Promontory shouted "fraud" and "blasphemy," stomping on the new pictures.

And it was then that the Commandant kicked out the deacons and turned the monastery into a prison.

III

THE
PROMONTORY

There on the Promontory, where the walls rose, narrowing, with heavy black cannons on their battlements, I saw the prisoners a day before they were taken to the quarry. They gave me all kinds of odd things they happened to have in their pockets: photos, sunglasses, pencils, stamps, a cigarette holder, an amulet . . . And they touched, touched incessantly my hands, my hair, my eyes. How rough their fingertips were from the stones they carried all day! I was growing desperate trying to recognize my father among them.

A man of about thirty looked like my father, but he said he wasn't. He wanted to give me his last ration of bread, and I took it.

"Go home now," he said, "and tell your mother that tomorrow will be a better day."

"Will you try to escape tonight?" I asked.

"I will certainly think about it," he whispered, trying to smile.

Years ago, when the Promontory was used as a prison by another enemy, someone equipped with a large umbrella had tried to escape by jumping over the stone wall all the way down to the sea. No one knew if his umbrella had turned inside out from the pressure, or if the enemy Coast Guard got him back, or if he drowned. Some said that even if his umbrella had held, he'd still have gone down too fast not to drown. The patrol boats were searching and searching. Others said that the wind blew so hard on that day that it carried the man far away, landing him on a rocky island, and that he stayed on that rock as a hermit for the rest of his life.

The prisoner who looked like my father smiled again. "Tomorrow will be a better day," he said, "one way or another," he said. "Make sure to be there."

"I will be there," I promised.

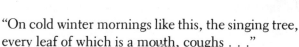

"On cold winter mornings like this, the singing tree, every leaf of which is a mouth, coughs . . ."

THE DAWN AND THE CITY

I opened my eyes and saw my father was already up, staring at the door, listening to the turn of the key. Once again I closed my eyes.

"Now, don't let them scare you, son. If I am not wrong, they'll just take us out for a breath of fresh air," he added.

When the door opened, I recognized the warden from his thick, irritated eyelids and the heavy ring of keys he held. There were also two military policemen armed with submachine guns, and a civilian who limped in a slight vertical motion. The civilian ordered us to get ready.

"We're going out for a breath of fresh air," he said.

My father and I looked at each other and smiled. We let the warden lock the handcuffs around our wrists. I closed my eyes again.

We rode in an armored truck, led and followed by motorcycles of the Military Police. Through the back window of reinforced glass, I saw the dawn and the city. Roads empty, stores shut. No milkmen, icemen, or trash collectors. The curled-up figure of a middle-aged man in the doorway of a public building. Another man, almost lost in a large overcoat, scavenged around a trash can. I saw the reflection of a stronger light at the tops of the tallest buildings. A salmon, liquid light. The city was still asleep, half dead. Outside of town, I saw sparse patches of grass and weed. Two crows hopped awkwardly, as if they couldn't fly. When the truck turned, my father pointed to the mountain.

"The quarry is abandoned like an outdoor theater in winter," he said. And he said, "This time of year the stage is always flooded."

The civilian uncuffed our wrists and ordered us to walk into the water. We walked until we reached the face of the rock. As soon as we turned around, the civilian, surrounded by five soldiers, began to read something I didn't understand. My father seemed to know.

"Don't let those beasts scare you now, son," he said calmly.

I took a deep breath and leaned against the rough surface of the rock. A few white clouds slowly turned pink, then dissolved in the blue of the sky. The sun was coming up fast. Any time now the city would be flooded with sudden light. I closed my eyes. Uncle Thanasis would be getting up now for his rounds in the neighborhoods, collecting all the bottles or fragments of glass he could find. Sometimes he even found pieces of lead, which was a great thing, as he said, because he could get good money for it. Suddenly I heard Uncle Thanasis' voice: "Aim!"

There were five soldiers stretching out their rifles, and I saw five small mouths, five dark zeros aiming at us. I took a deep breath and leaned against the rock, looking at my father. I thought he'd be embarrassed, but he only seemed distracted. I closed my eyes.

A woodsman had already gone to work in the dark of the grove nearby. Every few seconds, I heard the impact of his ax on a tree, accompanied by a "Ha!" He'd rolled up his sleeves, and, arching his back to gain momentum, he took a deep breath, then exhaled forcefully as he delivered the blow: "Ha!" I could see his face. The veins of his neck had begun to swell, and there were droplets of sweat on his brow and around his graying sideburns. As he swung the ax once more, and his body turned slightly to the right, his head turning right and back, I saw the corner of his eye looking at me. I counted the double sounds of his ax and breath while waiting to hear the tree falling with the familiar crashing noise. I stopped breathing. I felt my knees weakening, my legs trembling. I kept my eyes shut.

I saw my father fall back into the water, the circles around him widening black and red. What had happened? The soldiers ejected the empty cartridges from their weapons. What is this? I shouted, but there was no sound coming out of my mouth. The civilian got into the truck in a hurry while the soldiers accelerated their motorcycles, and, turning around, they drove off, leaving streams of smoke and dust in the air. I pulled my father out, spread his body on top of a smooth rock. He was taking short, quick breaths, which made the blood gush faster from his wounds. I ran my hands all over his chest, trying to stop the flow.

He cracked open his eyes and smiled. "What do you think you are doing?" he whispered. He was so young.

My face grew dry, my lips stiff.

"What are we going to do?" he whispered, his voice trembling.

I panicked. I stood up and began to walk backward away from him.

"Don't leave me yet," he said, covering his eyes.

I sat down, at a distance, until noon, and when my clothes had dried and I got up again, my father did not object to my returning home.

THE
FACE
OF
THE
ROCK

"Do you see that mountain under the blazing sun?" said Grandfather. "See how one dry rock leans against another, and the loose pieces come off, small piles of debris rising from the black water? Beneath the scarred face of that rock there is a composite face of all your ancestors. These mountains, rocks and ravines, pines and olive trees, and scruffy shrubs will never change, disengage themselves, repudiate their history. Trees with the rope marks of the hanged never grow fast enough to heal completely, and a marked tree will be marked again. Predictable, most of the time predictable, soon enough those merciful crows will cover all of it over. Are you listening to me?" he asked.

"Yes, Grandfather."

"They mine the stone by firing at the rock, and the ravines reverberate with rifle shots and moans," he went on. "They fire, scarring the face of the rock, and when we wake up in the morning our own bodies are brittle and have a smell of old flowers. What did you do this morning?" he asked me.

I was making his drawing while he talked, and when he finished I started to work on Uncle Iasson, my father's young brother. Uncle was twenty. Like my father, he had a light complexion. When he worked outdoors, his skin tanned, but his hair turned even lighter. My father's father sat in the shade most of the time, so his skin, his hair, and mustache were always white.

"Are you listening to me?" he asked.

"Yes, Grandfather."

"What did I just ask you?"

"What did I do this morning."

"Well?"

"I went to the quarry."

"What for?"

"To look for my father."

Grandfather turned and looked at Uncle Iasson.

"I didn't see him," I said.

"What did you do once you got there?" asked Uncle Iasson.

"I took my ax and went to the grove, pretending to chop wood, so I could see the prisoners when they were brought to the quarry."

"How many this time?" asked Uncle Iasson.

"Two. But only one of them took the last sacraments and the blindfold. After the enemy left, I looked into the ditch, and the same prisoner who had taken communion still twitched and quivered in the water. But he wasn't my father."

"Make no mistake. He too was ours," said Grandfather.

IV

Those who took to the mountain armed themselves with axes, bread knives, and adzes. They chose moonless nights, hoping to catch the enemy asleep. They struck with axes, bread knives, and adzes, and they returned to the mountain with rifles, pistols, automatic weapons, and hand grenades. But having to learn how to use the enemy's arms distressed them. The speed with which these weapons worked frightened them, and many went back to axes, bread knives, and adzes. Which the enemy dreaded. Before mounting an assault, they stopped at an ancient site and talked about the battles of the past, and how our great-grandfathers dealt with invaders from the East and from the West. They had written off their lives from the start, and each time they prepared for battle, they wished "fair bullet" and "fair death" to each other. The first Mountain Fighters were so generous with their lives that they sang and danced before battle, and often invited Death himself to choose one of them as a partner. First they blindfolded a fighter and put a loaded pistol in his hand. Then they began to dance in a circle around him. At the peak of the song, when the dancers rushed forward in a fury, leaping and threatening the earth by passing a hand through the grass, the man at the center fired the pistol, and one of the dancers was sent out of the circle of the dance and out of life. Grandmother said that her own grandfather, who was a notorious captain of the Mountain Fighters, had tried to ban the Dance of Death in his army, but even he had failed. At the end he was so mad at his men that he said to them, "I don't mind if you simpletons waste one of your kind from time to time, but I resent it like hell when you waste that bullet."

One evening, a friend of Grandmother's came to visit, and I had to sit in the pantry quietly. Grandmother's friend had already lost her husband and her first son, a mathematician, to enemy bullets. She was a symbol of defiance and sacrifice. People called her Aunt Liberty. According to a story, her son had been sitting under an oleander at noontime when he started shouting that he'd squared the circle.

AUNT LIBERTY HAS A PLAN

"Hard to explain," said Aunt Liberty. "All I can say is that people have been trying to square the circle for a long time, especially since somebody or other proved it's impossible."

He shouted that he'd squared the circle, and began to sing. Two enemy soldiers who happened to be driving by on a motorcycle stopped, took aim, and shot him. Aunt Liberty said that the bullet that hit her son had left a small black hole in the air next to the oleander. We never found out why they had killed him. The Commandant promised to conduct an investigation. Nobody believed him.

"Let God love the living," said Grandmother.

Aunt Liberty worried about Mikés, her younger son, who was sixteen and wanted to take revenge for his father and brother. The old woman tried to persuade him to do so by joining the Mountain

Fighters, but he wouldn't listen. He wanted to do it all by himself.

"His blood is crazy," complained Aunt Liberty. "What am I to do? I'm getting old; chances are I won't make it through this winter."

"That's nonsense," said Grandmother. "You're a strong old bone; you'll make it all right."

"But if I die, who's going to stop him from risking his own life in taking revenge?"

"He's old enough to know," said Grandmother.

"No, he's not old enough, and you don't understand what I mean," insisted Aunt Liberty.

"Well, what *do* you mean?"

"When I die, no one will be able to stop him, and chances are he'll get killed," whispered Aunt Liberty.

"What if he takes revenge and then joins the Mountain Fighters?"

"Ah, but what would his chances be of surviving that long?"

"Hard to tell," admitted Grandmother.

"That's why I thought of taking revenge myself," whispered Aunt Liberty. "I will soon die anyway," she added, "but if I can do it before I die, Mikés won't have to risk his own life for it."

"You must be out of your mind," said Grandmother.

BIRD
IN
EXILE

Just before my father was transferred from the Promontory, my mother went to plead with the authorities for his life. She was pregnant then, and the neighborhood women thought the Commandant might be moved and send my father home, or at least spare his life and send him to a labor camp. There had been stories in the past about this, there had been precedents: a young prisoner who happened to resemble a general's son was spared at the last moment and set free. A pregnant woman who was the namesake of another high officer's daughter had also been spared. But those high officers were not typical enemy officers, and Grandmother doubted that they were even real. "We just dream them up," she used to say. "When things get tough, we'll dream up anything, even a swine with angel wings." My mother never came back from the Promontory. When, the next day, Grandmother went to the Security Station to find out what had happened to my mother, the Commandant said that he hadn't seen her. Several weeks later we heard a rumor that she, having failed to save my father, went to join the Mountain Fighters. And then Lekas the Informer told someone or other that, according to his information, the doctor had been ordered to perform an abortion on my mother, which improved her qualifications for the labor camp. "That's probably true," said Grandmother. "Lekas is an insider; he knows what's going on." With the baby in her belly she would be useless to the enemy, the only other place for her would have been the quarry. Grandmother said that before my mother disappeared she had worried about her condition, about having to raise one more child without milk and medicine. Then Grandmother remembered my mother herself as a child, growing up sickly during an earlier war, and she began to weep and to chant a lament about a bird in exile, about apples that rot and quince that dry and shrivel. Whenever she chanted like that, she always lowered her black scarf over her wrinkled face, and I sat in the pantry quietly, listening to her and actually seeing all the things that she named.

FURTHER REPRISAL

For about two weeks after my mother disappeared, I continued to sleep in our own house rather than move to my grandmother's or to my paternal grandfather's. During the day I spent a few hours with each one, but in the evening I went to sleep in my own bed, to make sure that I wouldn't miss my parents if they decided to visit secretly in the night. From time to time, I heard voices or steps outside the house, and I ran to the window, hoping it might be they. I always returned to bed with their features confused in my mind, and I couldn't go back to sleep before piecing together the right eyes, noses, lips, and smiles on their faces. It was like making their drawings on cardboard for my shadow theater.

One evening I was late getting home, and I had difficulty opening the door. I turned the key, pressed down the latch, and pushed; but it wouldn't open. I pushed harder and heard the grinding sound of debris on the floor. I pushed still harder with my right arm and shoulder, forcing my way in. I looked around and realized with amazement that the rest of the house was missing. The roof, the walls, the partitions, the furniture, were no longer there. Only the front wall, the main door, and the floor still existed. All around I could see the trees in the yard, and the neighborhood. And when I looked up, I saw the changing sky: fast-moving clouds and the cold stars.

Next day I learned that the Commandant had sent a wrecking crew to tear down the house, in further reprisal. No one could explain why the front wall had been spared. I took it personally: the nasty joke of sparing the front wall and the door—that was the further reprisal. For a long time afterward, whenever I was about to open the door of a house, I closed my eyes and prepared myself to face another extraordinary landscape.

Our neighbors, Uncle Spanos and Aunt Zoë, who were brother and sister, treated me to a cup of camomile tea to console me for the loss of the house I was born in. Uncle Spanos, who used to be a fisherman before the enemy brought in the concrete ships and mined the bay, knew a lot of stories about the sea. Each time he told me one, I took my little notebook out and wrote down a few key words, which I later on used in my shadow theater episodes. Now Uncle Spanos wanted to tell me the story of the hermit crab, but Aunt Zoë thought this was hardly an occasion to tell stories. Uncle Spanos did not agree. "Every occasion is the right occasion, and every story is worth listening to," he said. Then Aunt Zoë excused herself, and I took out my pencil and notebook.

Do you know that seaweed glows at night? Who do you think lights it up, and from what, and who besides the hermit crab takes advantage of it? The seaweed has the light but doesn't need it; undulates in it but doesn't know it; and it wouldn't mind spending the night in the dark, or so it seems. Now no one takes credit for that glow, and no one can unmake it, and the fish gather about it curiously. Now the sponge absorbs more water because of it, and the coral's heart of stone throbs with life. Now the sand swells, and the hermit crab takes shelter, and someone is heard accusing him of murder and theft, of taking advantage of that glow, etc. But now, under that glow, while the coral throbs and the sponge gurgles, the hermit crab discovers the burdens of property.

V

THE DOCTOR OF HUNGER

The town doctor spent most of his time in bed, and the house calls were made by the patients. Anyone in need of medical advice and treatment had to visit the doctor at his bedside. "When there is nothing to eat for more than a week, you too should stay in bed and try to sleep as much as you can," he advised. "Sure, that prolongs the suffering," he said, "but it also preserves your last bit of energy, and you live longer. When worst comes to worst that's what I do, and that's as much advice as I can give to others," he said, "especially when it comes to elderly patients. But there's a problem with old people," he added. "Some of them live alone, and when they die in their beds no one knows it for days, sometimes for weeks, until their bodies decompose, and they're discovered by the stench, so there's always the danger of epidemic. . . . Like the epidemic that wiped out half of this town years ago, when I first came here as a young doctor."

The doctor's description of our town following that epidemic made me think of the painting in the small city hall, and his stories about the past always sounded familiar to me, even though they referred to a time long before I was born. I decided to add the doctor to my puppet collection, so I could expand my shadow theater repertory with an episode from that epidemic.

The town, a memory of mystery and melancholy. Empty the buildings with the endless rows of columns, arches, arcades. The midday sun blasting on the black cobblestones and the sculpture of the sleeping woman in the square. Serenity. A young swallow flew across the square, then perched on a large wooden crate on wheels that gathered dust by the dried-out fountain. Serenity. "That crate belonged to a troupe of actors who had visited here to perform in the open air," said the doctor. "When the epidemic broke out, several superstitious people, encouraged by the priest, spread a rumor that it was the theater group that had brought the disease. The priest then suggested throwing the actors into a ditch brimming with boiling limestone, which would disinfect them before killing them. The actors disappeared the following night, leaving everything behind: stage sets, costumes, and crate. The priest said that the actors had run in order to save their skins and to spread the disease elsewhere." The doctor leaned against the sculpture of the sleeping woman, scratching his head. "How could they spread the disease but still save their own skins?" he asked. For many years a strange serenity settled together with the dust in the square. Sometimes during the night, those who had survived the epidemic could hear voices in the square, dialogue, laughter, cries, and they'd open the windows, expecting to see the actors perform, but the actors were never seen again. During the day, from the half-opened door of that crate, poured forth a black velvet light.

The next time I saw the doctor, he talked about something else, something more scary: the Security Station. "It's hard to tell what the Security Forces secure, from whom, and in whose name," said the doctor, lowering his voice. "They said that the man they dragged in last night probably works as a spy for the terrorists who call themselves Mountain Fighters, and the Commandant ordered his officers and the informers to interrogate him and get a full confession. But I doubt the prisoner had anything to do with the Mountain Fighters," said the doctor. "The Mountain Fighters just don't get caught—not alive. In any case, this one wouldn't speak. He wouldn't admit to being a spy or an anarchist, so they took him down to the basement and beat him up. They used rubber hoses and lead pipes, which can break the bones without bruising the skin. To cover his cries, they turned on a motorcycle in the same room. . ."

I had heard many stories about torture before, and I always wondered about that motorcycle and why they accelerated it during beating sessions. Why did they try to cover up the victim's cries? Was it to deprive the prisoner even of the hope that someone outside might hear him and sympathize with him? Or was it because the torturers hated to hear the cries?

"Neither," said the doctor. "They don't know this, but the victim's cries remind them of their own silent cries."

"Do they torture even themselves?"

"Yes, without knowing it. That's why their own crying is silent."

That evening I brought up the subject with Grandmother. "Why is their own crying silent? Is it because they don't know that they're torturing themselves?"

"No," said Grandmother, "it's silent because they're not torturing themselves hard enough."

Then Grandmother talked about the Mountain Fighters. "The Mountain Fighters are as hungry as we are, but they don't have to bend their necks to the enemy," she said. "They're pursued and hunted day and night by enemy soldiers, informers, and dogs, but they're never caught—not alive. They have no priest to bless their arms, no doctor, and no medicine to heal the wounds they suffer." And she said, "The women don't wash, don't cook, don't go to bed with the men. The women wear trousers and heavy shirts, and cartridge belts over their breasts. They clip their hair short to fit workmen's caps, and in the night their lovers are their knives and rifles. Enemy soldiers and informers dread the women fighters more than the men. They often talk about trapping, catching them, but so far they haven't caught one—not alive. These women don't worship any god, and the informers call them whores," said Grandmother. "That's because when they swear at the enemy, even the men who fight alongside them blush. And many men worry that if the struggle lasts a few more years, family life won't be the same again. But altogether, they're glad to see how wise in strategy and how brave in battle their women are, and when a man's opinion stands out, the others praise him by saying, 'He's got a woman's mind.' The Mountain Fighters are as hungry as we are," said Grandmother, "but when they lean against a rock holding their rifles, their eyes squint as they try to focus on something very small and very distant, something that grows and changes day by day, and is completely invisible to us living in town."

THE
SECURITY
STATION

The next morning, when I passed by the Security Station and heard the deafening noise of the motorcycle coming from the basement, it sounded to me as though a man had actually been imprisoned in a motorcycle engine. I stood there, unable to go forward or to turn back—my knees shaking, my legs numb. Suddenly, one of the informers, who'd seen me from the window, came out and ordered me to move along. I tried to move but couldn't. He pushed me to get going.

"That man inside the motorcycle engine is my father," I said.

He slapped me with the back of his hand, and I fell down. "Even dead, your old man's too big to fit inside that motor," he said, laughing. "Now move along, or I'll have to lock you up."

I spent that morning in jail.

"How do you recognize a spy?" I asked the informer sitting at the desk.

"From the way he looks at people and things," he said. "A spy's always looking around military installations, often corrupting officials with money or blackmail, and keeping a record of what he learns in a little book with secret words."

I remembered my little notebook. I reached for it in my pocket, but it wasn't there. I was lucky not to have carried it on me that day. The informer was sitting outside my cell, sipping coffee and smoking. The beating downstairs had stopped a while ago. The informer who sat outside my cell was a young man from a neighboring town. He seemed nervous.

Each time he lifted the coffee cup to his lips, his hand shook, causing the cup and the saucer to rattle. When he became aware of my eyes, he put the cup on his desk.

"It's not easy to try and make someone talk," he said, grinning.

"He's my father," I said.

"What?"

"What I said."

"The kid's a pathological liar," said Lekas, who had just walked in and overheard me. "Come along," he said to me, opening the door. "Come see for yourself."

I was surprised. I wasn't prepared for such attention, and I wasn't sure whether or not I wanted to see the prisoner. I held on to the bars, trying to think, but Lekas dragged me out and forced me down a narrow stair to the basement. We stopped in front of a tin-paneled door. He unlocked it and pushed it open. It was dark in there. I took a cautious step forward, then quickly I stepped back. The floor of the small cell was flooded. It was part of an old method of breaking the prisoner by making it impossible for him to lie down and rest between the beating sessions. But here it didn't seem to work. The prisoner was probably so badly hurt that he couldn't stand on his feet, and at some point he had just collapsed. As my eyes became increasingly accustomed to the dark, I began to see the prisoner more clearly. The water did not cover his face. His body was curled up, his head resting on his shoulder. There was blood trickling from his nose, blood spreading in wide slicks on the water. From time to time he twitched, which made me think that he was asleep and having terrible dreams. His shirt was torn in several places, and bloodied. His feet were tied together onto a small metal rack which raised them well above the water, and his soles were so swollen that they looked round. There was a sour smell of vomit, mixed with other odors from the piss and shit he could no longer hold.

"Well," said Lekas.

I couldn't answer. My mouth was slowly filling with the thin saliva that comes before vomiting.

"Is this your old man?" asked Lekas.

Had I been able to speak, I would have said, "How can I be sure?" But instead, I threw up on his shirt.

VI

A week or so before, the doctor had thought that
Aunt Liberty was losing her sanity, but Grandmother said it wasn't anything serious. Then the
Commandant ordered Mikés not to let his mother
out of the house anymore, because her condition
might disturb the public order. The truth was that
Aunt Liberty had been overheard by the informers
saying that the Archangel was about to descend
with his flaming sword upon the foreign locust—
whatever that meant. When she was told not to
leave the house anymore, Aunt Liberty didn't seem
to mind, but when Mikés went out later that day,
she took the ikon of the Archangel from its shelf,
and her old man's dagger, which she'd kept under
the mattress, and she made for the church.

I saw her in the street, saw her scarf and her long
gray hair flowing behind her—you'd think a sudden
gust of wind had risen from the bay in the dead of
the noon hour, so forceful her stride was—and her
eyes, fixed on the blue dome of the belltower, were
serene and determined. I wondered what sort of
instinct had made me turn and look at the deserted
street from the window. I turned, and there she
was, dark against the wind, her Archangel serene,

and her dagger determined. I ran after her in the white street, followed her to the church, and when she knelt and crossed herself in the churchyard, I hid behind the dry wall and waited. Short prayer, Aunty Liberty stood up. "Yes," I heard her cry. "Yes, I listen and obey!" She crossed herself and headed for the Security Station, right at the end of the street. I slowed down, and as she approached the building, I hid behind a fence. Then when I peeked around the corner, I saw Aunt Liberty climb up the three steps quickly and kick the door of the Station in. I saw her walk right in, holding the Angel against her bosom, raising her dagger. I closed my eyes, closed my eyes and listened, and heard a shout and a shot, then the echo of the shot and the shout.

THE END OF THE SPY

Next morning Grandmother and I went to see the doctor about Aunt Liberty. We found him in bed with cold compresses on his forehead.

"Yes, she's gone," he confirmed. "When I got there, the old woman lay on the floor, in a pool of brains and blood. Crazy, just crazy. . ."

"That's what I thought too, but I was wrong," said Grandmother. "She knew what she was doing."

"I hadn't gone there to see her," said the doctor without listening to Grandmother. "They had dragged me over to the Station to try and do something for the young guy they'd worked on. I didn't know where to start. So I asked how he was feeling. I think he was trying to smile. All his front teeth were gone, and as he breathed through the mouth he made a bubble with his blood—such a smile!"

"Doctor, you have a temperature," said Grandmother, taking his pulse.

"I told them, told them again that this time they went too far, that there wasn't much I could do for the prisoner," said the doctor, paying no attention to Grandmother. "They laughed in my face, saying, 'Come on, we didn't bring you here to do something for him, but for your country. Clean him up! Give him a shot to revive him! We're not through with him yet."

"What did you do then, Doctor?" asked Grandmother.

"I cleaned him up, tried to stitch him back together. His skin was so badly damaged that it tore like paper. Suddenly he opened his eyes, twitched, then fell into a coma again. Later on they managed to bring him around for a while with electric shock, but I guess he never confessed, never named names or anything."

"Thank God," said Grandmother, crossing herself.

"Not that he was brave, or particularly stubborn, mind you," the doctor went on. "No, he was quiet by nature. A shepherd from the hills, I think, and a pretty dumb one too, I should add. Because if he'd pretended to know something and said it, he might have saved his skin—I mean, literally. Oh, well. This morning they said they'd found him hanged. They said he used his belt and a hook on the ceiling, and hanged himself. Hard to swallow that one. Especially since he did not have a belt, since there was no hook or anything on the ceiling, and since he couldn't stand on his feet. This morning they asked me to go back to the Station and confirm their story in writing, but I stayed home sick."

The funeral service for Aunt Liberty was brief, and there was no service at all for the prisoner who had been found hanged in his cell. Since according to the official announcement the prisoner had taken

THE
SINGING
TREE

his own life, the priest refused to perform the last rites before burial, saying that suicide is an unpardonable sin. We took the body out of town to the hills; we took it and buried it under an oak tree. Among the people who had followed the procession were two women I hadn't seen for a long time: Xanthi, who used to be a prostitute and now lived in the abandoned crate in the town square; and the old retired teacher, who delivered memorable eulogies. When the body of the prisoner, wrapped in a white bedsheet, was lowered into the grave, she told us the parable of the singing tree.

"Death is ephemeral," she said, "but that doesn't make life eternal. Once there was a pomegranate tree in full blossom, and in one of its flowers there was a bee. The bee started to walk around the lip of the flower cone, sizing up the narrow mossy tube of its throat. The bee heard music coming from within the flower, and a voice singing, 'Come closer, rub your wings on my lips, and I'll kiss you back, with honey and with fragrance.' The bee took a few more steps. The translucent moss of the flower's tube sloped inward. Already she could breathe the fragrance, but the honey was deeper in. 'Come in, little bee,' sang the tree, and the bee slipped right in, brushing her delicate wings against the reeds that followed her, stretching their tiny free ends after her. At the end of the long tunnel, she stepped down into a small greenish puff. The light came in palely through the veined membrane, making the droplets of honey look like frost. Once she had gathered as much nectar as she could carry, the bee leaped to the narrow portal of the tunnel, but the moss was still blowing inward, and the passage itself had contracted. The bee inspected the wall, went back to the portal, walked and flew back and forth. There was no exit. The green sack grew quiet, grew dark. Without the air from outside, the fragrance became so strong that the bee thought she would faint. She licked her legs, remained still, rested. Her eyes were like two droplets of honey. All around her silence, and a greenish dusk. Her sight grew dim, she began to perspire, she seemed to fall asleep. Slowly, the veins of the sack turned pink, then the whole pomegranate tree shivered and began to sing. The puff contracted, tightening the arches of its tendons, and expanded, shaking violently. The bee awoke. Then the passage began to expand too, filling the little globe with clean air, and a beam of direct light passed through the parting reeds, turning the interior gold. The bee leaped to the smooth ring of the exit and dashed out into the bright air."

The old teacher looked at us standing around the grave mesmerized, and she smiled. "Cover the body," she said. "Death is ephemeral; life is not forever."

Philippos, Flisvos, and I decided to find out more about the dead, and we went to ask Grandmother. She didn't feel like talking. All she could tell us was that the earth is a huge green puff, and in the middle of that puff there is an island surrounded by a sea of honey. The dead are invisible. They stay in an old mansion on that island, and then once in a while a tunnel opens up, and the dead find their way back here, just like the bee the old teacher talked about.

THE
REALM
OF
DEATH

"Once they find their way back here, are they still invisible?" asked Flisvos.

"No, they are not invisible," said Grandmother, "but they don't look the way they used to, either."

"How do they look, Grandma?"

"They look different."

After Flisvos and Philippos had left, I asked her to tell me once and for all the story behind the singing trees.

"That's a long story," she said.

"The pomegranate tree sang just before the bee went into the puff, and then again before she found her way out," I said.

"That ought to answer your question," she said.

"How?"

"When a tree sings, it's because somebody dies, or because somebody comes back from the dead."

"But are the trees real, Grandmother?"

"Like everything else, it depends on how you look at it."

THE
MANSION
BENEATH
THE
SEA

Uncle Spanos, who knew all about the sea and the islands, was more talkative. He didn't know anything about the earth being a huge green puff. "But yes, islands do sink from time to time," he said. He spoke of contours, levels, and what he called the Ultimate Elevation, where the seaweed undulates and the fish get dizzy. "Honey? That's nonsense," he said. And he said, "It's water, blue water, so blue that it dyes your toes; and the surface of the sea is only one of many surfaces. The sand before the pebbles, the stones that follow floating, and the rock with the deep imprint of a fisherman's foot—that old a rock," he said. "Dry walls saddled with tumbleweeds that make the wind whistle, and fearless trees with a braid of garlic between their legs spread skyward. The one-room house, and the other house lost in the sky and below the water—

that's the mansion you're talking about, isn't it? Well, that house is so high you have to dye your toes in the sea and the sky the second time to reach it. Have you seen its entrance? A gate by the mountain, by the white wall, a lighted well and a corridor, smooth pebbles darker at the turn of the tree, wrought-iron chairs around the tree now closing in. Paint chip, metal blood. The cactus grew in proportion, outgrew their prediction, October the well overflowed and the cactus collapsed, a column of water. Amaryllis the Wild," he said. "Amaryllis a gust of wind, an explosion of seeds. No birds before the window, no shadows beyond, left and right an echo of steps and a smell of tobacco. Who's minding the mansion and the mountain? Whose vein is draining when the lip of the cliff bleeds? When the ocean darkens, whose steps can leave an imprint on water? Steps again, then a ramp, a wall at the end, now a turn, steep ramp, then another flight of stairs, then water. Sometimes, when the brain is bleeding, that vein is rejoicing," he said.

VII

Just before the enemy confiscated our male goat, Grandmother sent me to bring him home from a farm nearby. Pan was a strong, proud goat. Shining light brown coat with white patches on his chest and rump, and big horns spiraling twice over his head like a crown. He had a pointed reddish beard and a powerful odor. He'd spent the last couple of days at that farm at stud. The female goats belonged to a middle-aged woman whom people called the Deaf One. She was not deaf. She could hear perfectly well but had the nasty habit of talking all the time, so she never listened to what others had to say to her. Besides her "deafness," she had a reputation for playing games on people, and when Grandmother sent me over to get our goat, she warned me to be on the lookout for tricks. When I got to the farmhouse, the Deaf One was in the back yard feeding the chickens. As soon as she saw me, she rushed into the barn, and a minute later she appeared holding in her arms a newborn kid whose coat looked very much like Pan's.

"Look what I've got for you," she said. "Well, aren't you and your grandma the luckiest! But why didn't she tell me that your goat was pregnant? Don't tell me, I'll guess. Let me see now. . . . Your grandma was embarrassed to admit a thing like that—right? Who wouldn't be?"

Once she started to talk, it became clear that a trick was in progress. She went on and on. "Here, take this little one to your grandma," she said. "Legally it belongs to her. And tomorrow, after the church service, when the lucky father is better, you can also take him back. Yes? As for my hot young lady goats, I guess I'll have to look for a stud that— Oh, never mind; just take this little one home. God," she sighed as she walked toward the chickens, "some people are so lucky, even their he-goats get pregnant."

"Now let me put two and two together," said Grandmother. "If she's going to find another stud, it means she won't be paying us the stud fee, and that figures. On the other hand, she's letting us have the kid, which *is* the stud fee we agreed on. I don't get it," she said. "Well, maybe she's not out for trpicks this time; maybe she's just joking. On the other hand—No, I bet there's more to it than that."

"What can it be, Grandmother?"

"Say that tomorrow, when you go to get our Pan, the Deaf One announces to you that he grew wings and flew off, or something. If we buy one miracle, how can we refuse to buy another?"

Next morning I woke up with the sound of the church bell. Grandmother was already up, standing by the window.

"Grandma, aren't you going to wear your Sunday dress for the service?"

"Today we'll do something else to spite the Devil," she said without turning her face from the window.

"What are you looking at?" I asked.

"Sh . . . I'm waiting to see the Deaf One going to church."

"What for?"

51

"Wash your face and put on your clothes. We're going to visit the Deaf One's house before she gets back from church."

"What makes you think that she'll go to church?"

"Ha! If thieves and hypocrites stayed away, the churches would be empty on Sundays," she said.

Half an hour later Grandmother and I were sneaking into the Deaf One's barn, where we found Pan and a young female goat tied to the same pole.

"Let's take him and go," I said impatiently.

"Sh . . . Not yet," said Grandmother. "Look."

Pan had begun to sniff and lick the young goat, then sniff again and make funny faces and rise on his hind legs. The female goat was alarmed and ran around the pole away from him, not knowing that there was an end to her line. Pan pawed the ground, snorting, and took a few more steps after her.

"You just can't stop him now," said Grandmother.

Pan followed the little goat step by step, sniffing her, licking her, his prick already unfolding, red, long, and threaded, with a tip like a small carnation. Both lines were soon wound around the pole. Pan stopped to watch the other go to the very end, her head against the pole, her forelegs forced to kneel. Pan lowered his own head and let a stream of steaming spray go forward and up, sprinkling his face. He set out for the final assault while she stood immobile, with nothing but a nervous tail for defense. Once again he rose on his hind legs, then jumped her, sliding right into her, and—damn! It always happened so fast I never could see exactly how he got around that tail.

When the enemy soldiers put him onto the truck with the other confiscated animals, Grandmother couldn't hold back her tears; but Pan, having recognized the Deaf One's little goat in the crowd, went right after her again for the last time.

Night away from home, night on the long road, the horse exhausted and the old wagon breaking down. George must be out of his mind to have kept going day and night, from town to town, without having anything to sell or to trade. He must have hoped to get something for the family, a sack of grain or a can of olives from a town that's richer than ours. It's hard to go home with empty hands, but how can you buy something without money? Besides, the houses that still had grain in their cellars were double-locked, and the old people who lived in them were scared and looked like ghosts. They wouldn't even greet a stranger. George sat down by the roadside, stroking his horse's brow. "When the war started and the enemy confiscated the youngest one of my horses, I thought I'd give up traveling and do something else for a living, but I couldn't come up with anything," he said. "I am used to this, you see. It's my job, my trade. It makes sense to me, even if I can't make a living at it anymore. As for the horse, if I had a choice I'd still stick with this one. He's such a hard worker, such a pal. It'd be ungrateful of me to hand him over to the enemy because he's getting old. The enemy, you see, doesn't understand people or animals, and this one's a member of the family—a brother. Would you give away your brother? In the old days I had only one horse—him. We'd travel together doing business throughout the southern part of the country, where the earth's more generous, and see towns and places that others only hear about, and we'd always return weeks later with all kinds of goods and stories. Sure we never made much profit, but there was enough bread and wine on the table, and warm clothes for the winter. He was a proud horse, a noble animal, but now . . ." Night away from home, night on the long road, night of the horse struggling and failing, night of the horse dying. George spent the night on the roadside talking to the horse, trying to help him up, or stroking his brow, retelling old stories that the animal should still remember. Have you ever seen an old horse struggling for the last time to stand up, and failing? George stood up, sat down again, embraced the horse's long neck. Quietly he began to weep. And at daybreak the animal shook a couple of times, and it was dead. And George couldn't decide to go back home or anywhere else.

The blind man stroked the head of his dog, and continued to talk without playing his guitar: "As I passed, the crows flew off, uncovering the carcass of the horse, and hovered above us, waiting—the carcass an unfinished boat. The days ahead of us are being finished for us by crows. I sat down and sang most of the night, all night, and when the sharp wind of the sea reached me at dawn, my heart was still crying."

COMMUNION

I sat at the window sill, trying to see through the frost. Is that a sparrow? A breath of icy air crept across my eyes. I saw him landing from the fig tree, scratching the ice for food. And then I saw the shadows of the bare branches surrounding him. The sparrow was skinny but felt warm as I touched him to my cheek. "What do you know?" I tapped his little hard head, asked him, "What do you know about hunger?" He cracked open his beak, letting out a small cry. "I don't know either," I said. He pecked at my hand. His tongue and the inside of his mouth were like a tiny silver and gold spoon, the spoon the priest used to give the communion with. Warmer in my hands, he started to close his eyes. "Go to sleep, it's nothing." I closed my own eyes, but my fingers continued to see. I worried that the fluttering of my eyelids might wake him. Quickly I twisted his neck full circle until I felt his tiny spine snap. End of heartbeat. My hands felt dry and stiff like winter trees. I saw a light coming down through branches, and for a moment the glitter of the ax whistling among the shadows. A spasm in my own neck, but it passed. I plucked the sparrow, touched the last warmth of his blood. I gutted him, broke his ribcage open, flattened him. Quickly onto the fire, a minute or so each side. The ends of his ribs crisped, the blood, his little blood, turning to juice, and dripping. And then it was my mouth embracing the sparrow. I was warmer, my throat was warmer, as if I had taken in his voice, and had been singing with it for hours.

VIII

CAPETAN
PERSEUS

For the sake of security, every leader of the resistance assumed a pseudonym, to which a Mountain Fighter would attach the title "Capetan." In our region, the first rebel leader to become well known was Capetan Perseus, the name originally of another local hero. But Capetan Perseus wasn't armed with the so-called three magical S's, which stood for Shield, Sword, and Sandals, so the monsters trapped him alone one day. They wanted him alive. First they shot at him and wounded both his arms, so he couldn't fire back, and then his legs so he couldn't escape. Capetan Perseus was writhing in the dust, pleading with anyone who might be nearby to finish him off so he wouldn't be taken alive, but the only one who heard him was unarmed, and the enemy sergeant and two of his men were already closing in on their victim. What could I do? In a few seconds they'd have him in their hands alive. But then I saw Capetan Perseus roll over, face down, and remain still. The enemy soldiers reached him and tried to lift him up. Instead, they lifted up an explosion. I saw it, I ducked down to hide from the shrapnel, and when I looked up again I saw the bodies of all four men strewn around, torn to pieces, some of the limbs twitching. What had happened? How did it happen? Some said that the original Perseus had heard the plea of his namesake and pitied him and delivered a shell, another of his magical S's, blowing up the hero as well as the monsters. Others explained the episode differently. They said that because Capetan Perseus' head was blown to such tiny bits and pieces, he must have turned around at the last moment to cover a hand grenade with his face, and to pull off the firing pin with his teeth.

When the news about Capetan Perseus' death reached the mountain, the men and the women of his band gathered around his wife to console her. She stopped them at the first word.

"Had he allowed himself to be caught alive, I might have had use for your sympathy," she shouted, raising her rifle. "Not only did he not get caught, he took three of the others with him. This then is an occasion to celebrate rather than to mourn. Remember his example," she said. "And don't expect me to weep for anyone, or to have use for anyone else's tears, unless we lose this war."

They listened quietly, then fired off three barrages to honor the death of Capetan Perseus, and swore to take back his blood. Later they danced to old mountain songs of freedom, and in the evening they chose the hero's widow to be their new leader. She had black hair, pale dark skin, and gray eyes. She was a small woman. She didn't talk very much, but when she did talk, the Mountain Fighters said that her words had weight. When she was teased about being so small and skinny, she said, "If I were any bigger, I wouldn't live to see so many bullets go by me." The day she was chosen to be the chief of the Mountain Fighters, one of them remembered the woman of the ancient Perseus, and suggested

Andromeda as the war name of the new Capetan. She didn't care for it. She said she liked the first part of it, the "Andro," but she had no use for the rest. She finally picked Andromache, that name of a homeric heroine which meant "Fighter of Men."

IX

Summer fields: thistle and dry weed. The leftovers of straw, sharp, glittering in the strong light. It wasn't easy to cross summer fields without shoes. Grandfather, Uncle Iasson, and myself, three generations of barefoot walkers, had to sit down and help each other with little foot operations, using a pin, or a knife's point. The soles of our feet were tough, but not completely immune to thorns and sharp stones. We were on our way to the hills to search for food and for news about my parents. Whenever we stopped to get rid of a thorn and to rest, Uncle and I listened to Grandfather relate old stories that helped us to forget our hunger. We were looking forward to the better times that made such stories possible. Grandfather's favorite one was about the time he was young and handsome—and how he stood out as a reasonable man when confronted with the stupid brute force of a notorious bandit. After his having impressed the bandit with his gentle, civilized ways, the wild man became remorseful, begged forgiveness, and sought his friendship. But Grandfather wouldn't accompany the bandit on his frequent visits to the local whorehouse, and their friendship never became intimate.

OF
RED-
HAIRED
WOMEN

Then a pretty red-haired woman fell in love with Grandfather. She followed him wherever he went, disregarding the gossip. Grandfather loved to kiss her and stroke her long strawberry hair, but she was a passionate woman, he said, and when he refused to make love to her, she got a job in the whorehouse to spite him. Later on, she was carried off to the mountains to become the bandit's exclusive mistress. Grandfather said that red-haired women are special. You can't find many in this country, he said, but there have been several of them in our family already, and chances are there will be more.

A
STORY
PARTLY
TOLD

"Ah, to wake up on a late spring morning and take to the country," sighed Grandfather. "To take your time finding the path you knew years ago when you explored the woods, the marshes, and the riverbanks. To make your way through a field of wheat disturbed by wildflower bursts!"

"Were there real trees and water then, Grandfather?"

It must have been May. Grandfather touched the stalks of wheat, parted them, and there, right by his shadow, a young woman lay asleep, stark naked. "When she opened her eyes and saw me, she just smiled at me, saying, 'My legs and breasts are bruised from the poppies.' What do you answer to that—'I am sorry'? And then her face was covered with a scarf for a long time," said Grandfather. "Did I see her walk away, the stalks of wheat following her? Did she sit at the table saying, 'I'm late'? And did she say that again when she was leaving, before she went home for supper? Her mother stroked her hair while she ate, and later again while she slept. That scarf kept hiding her face for a long time," said Grandfather.

But things had changed a lot since the last time Grandfather was there. The tree was a little further to the left than he thought, and a cabin that belonged to an old blind lady was no longer there. "I wonder what ever happened to her little granddaughter with the bright blue eyes and the long hair the color of strawberry," said Grandfather. And he said, "Your father used to know her well."

"He did?"

". . . There used to be wild geese, and the trees were always wet. Once, while wandering around here, I heard distant thunder, and it occurred to me that I was lost."

Grandfather wouldn't say how my father knew the blind lady's granddaughter. The storm was only minutes away—but then what? Did it get dark all of a sudden? Did he seek cover under a large oak, trembling at the thought of lightning? Or did he find the cabin and sleep there for hours, tossing with disturbing dreams? Did a little voice wake him up? The rain had stopped, but it was still dark out there. My father could hear the grains of wheat sprout in the damp air with small explosions.

We saw her in the distance, moving cautiously among the thistles, her hair a reddish gold above the thistles, and through the thistles a ripple, her slender white body. As she approached, the distance seemed to increase rather than to shorten, and Uncle Iasson placed his hand above his eyes for shade.

"It's the light again, distorting everything," he said.

Her legs were scratched bloody by the thistles.

NO
ONE
POORER
THAN
I

She sat between me and Uncle Iasson, wiping her sweating brow with her arm. Dry leaves and thorns had caught in her long hair, and her light clothes were torn in several places. Deep blue eyes, pale skin. Her lips were chapped, with thin red cracks which she licked now and then. She started to say something, but changed her mind.

"Only when I heard thunder, did it occur to me that I was lost," said Grandfather. "That's because the landscape changes when the weather is rainy."

Uncle Iasson and I were staring at the woman. Slowly, she leaned back on her elbows.

"I don't know where I come from, or where I am going," she said, leaning back on her elbows. "I am lost even though the weather is not rainy," she said. "That's because I am so hungry, I guess," she said.

"You've come to the wrong town, my child," sighed Grandfather without looking at her. There was a tone of compassion in his voice, not only for her but for all of us.

"I am hungry, old man," she said again, looking at me this time.

"It's true, we have no bread," said Uncle Iasson, blushing.

"Only the enemy has bread," added Grandfather; "the enemy and his dogs."

"I'd do anything," said the woman, resting her cheek on the back of her hand.

"You've come to the wrong people," said Grandfather. "We are as poor as you are."

She shook her head. The dry leaves in her hair rustled, and as some of them changed places, she picked one that she could feel touching her neck, and offered it first to my uncle and then to me, confusing us. I took the leaf, and my uncle blushed.

"No one is poorer than I," she said softly; "no one."

Deep in the marshes, deep in the damp forest where wild ducks and geese lowered their wings, the water was still, and the water lilies bloomed and rotted at the same time. "And what kind of day will this be, my precious?" asked the blind lady. "Well, the cloud is glowing, it looks like rain, Grandmother." When my father passed by this place years ago, the little girl invited him in and washed his tired feet. "You don't hear of this kind of hospitality nowadays—not to mention the walnuts and honey that she treated him to later," said Grandfather. And in the evening, she took off her clothes and danced for him while the blind old woman recited stories from the Bible. "Where are you my child? What are you doing now?" she'd ask at the end of each story and dance. "Here, Grandmother. I am taking a breath before I start again," the little one would answer, and pull away from him.

Allow time to pass, and with time the tortured head will rest on the ancient wisdom of the shoulder and will learn. But time goes by so slowly that the landscape doesn't seem to change. And many more of these trees would have walked away if they had not been burdened with the dead weight of so many men. How did people come to think death by hanging dishonorable? Why was their last wish the quarry?

My father got a job at the quarry, and on payday he would climb down the hill to the cabin, carrying all kinds of presents for her. One time, the little red-haired girl asked him to spend the whole night with her, on condition that they wouldn't tell the old woman, and he accepted reluctantly.

"One can still climb up that quarry," said Grandfather. The face of the rock has rusted, its veins broken beneath the rust. Rains, wind, and landslides from the treeless mountainside try year after year to fill the dark scar, to no avail. The quarry workers, buried in the muck knee-high, remain unpaid, rusting but hardening like the rock itself.

"What happened during the rest of the night? How did that long night go by?"

"The light of your long life may never obscure the memory of the quarry workers," said Uncle Iasson, helping Grandfather up.

BRIEF BESTIARY

"Grandfather, is it true that storks feed their chicks with small hunks of their skin which they pluck from their own breasts?"

"I think it is," said Grandfather.

"What about the rats that get caught by the leg in a mousetrap, and bite off that whole leg to get away?" asked Uncle Iasson.

"You never know what an animal will do for dear life," said Grandfather.

"Then there's a spider called Black Widow which kills and devours her lover after mating," said Uncle Iasson.

"Can you imagine her killing him before?" said Grandfather.

"And I've heard of whales and dolphins that commit suicide," I said.

"Maybe when they're young and crazy," said Grandfather. And he said, "What's the matter with you two, anyway? Can't you find something more interesting to talk about?"

"There is a secret about each one of these things that I'd like to know before it's too late," said Uncle Iasson.

"There are some secrets that you can't learn before it's too late," said Grandfather.

64

"Is it true too that salamanders eat up their own tails in their effort to form a perfect zero?" I asked.

"Lizards are harmless even to themselves," said Grandfather. "And when they appear on house walls, people take it as a sign of good fortune for the household. And children never throw stones at them as they do with snakes. They only wish to catch a lizard by the tail, play with it for a while, then let go of it. Haven't you ever wanted to do that? But when you manage to grab one, the little creature tries to escape, and it pulls away so hard that its tail comes off. You become guilty and scared. You drop the severed tail to the ground, while the rest of the lizard creeps away as fast as it can. But the tail continues to writhe in the dust for a long time, as if it's struggling to find the rest of itself. This is the story behind each tailless lizard that you see when you lift a stone in a dry field in July or August."

"But what if it doesn't lose its tail? What about its trying to form that small perfect zero?"

"That small perfect zero is a big disturbing question," said Grandfather.

X

Soon after the death of Aunt Liberty, her son
Mikés, who was the last surviving member of that
family, went into hiding, and everyone knew that
he was planning his revenge. The informers
laughed it off but then began to worry. They urged
the Commandant to do something about it before
it was too late, but he could not understand.

"What do you mean, too late?" he asked. "Isn't it
true that he is only sixteen?"

"It's true, all right," said Lekas the Informer. "At
sixteen he's an adult. And when an adult pledges
to take revenge, he'll keep his word, or be
dishonored."

"What happens if he's dishonored?" asked the
Commandant.

"He dies. Usually by his own hand," said Lekas.

"Dishonor him," said the Commandant.

Lekas was disappointed. "Can we at least fire in
self-defense?" he asked.

"You can always fire in self-defense," said the
Commandant.

"That's all we wanted to hear," said Lekas, wink-
ing at the other informers.

A couple of weeks went by, and the informers

hadn't made any progress. In the meantime, Mikés began to gain the reputation of a daredevil. That made Lekas sick to his stomach. His efforts to find Mikés became so frantic that he even encouraged rumors about near-captures: how they'd almost got Mikés' ass, but at the last moment he'd slipped out of their hands, and such. The people, afraid even to mention his name, referred to him as the Unnamed One, which is a euphemism for the Devil. All kinds of stories about him, stories of extraordinary valor, spread rapidly: he'd steal food from the enemy, and give it to the hungry; he'd be surrounded, and he'd fight with his bare hands, unafraid of bullets; he was invisible, maybe even immortal. Only the old women refused to take part in such talk. When the name "Unnamed One" came up, they just shook their heads and wished that he'd keep out of Lekas' path.

No one hated mice more than the enemy. Women were afraid of mice, and often screamed when they saw one in the house. Men disliked them, but were amused when women screamed. Children found them interesting, although they were warned that rodents are carriers of disease. Cats loved to play with them and occasionally ate them. But no one hated mice more than the enemy did, and that's because they reminded him of people: small, stupid, powerless, hungry, miserable people. The smaller and hungrier the people, the greater the hate of the enemy. "Out of my way, you stupid little mouse," the enemy would say, kicking you in the ass. But if he were really angry at you, then it would be "Come here, you rat, let me see your tail."

We were small and frightened like mice. We were also contaminated, and we menaced the enemy by trying to get to his supplies. That made us rats. Because once we got to his food, we ate some, stole

RODENTS

67

some, and made a mess of the rest of it. The enemy had more names for us. Depending on the circumstances, we were dogs, worms, lizards, sheep, cows—anything. Anything but swine, which is what we called the enemy, usually behind his back.

As food supplies disappeared from our households, so did the mice and rats, and in the second year of the famine, seeing a mouse around was a good sign. All the rodents that abandoned us when we lost our food to the enemy simply followed the enemy and took up residence in the school building, where he kept his provisions. And that turned out to be an unending menace to the enemy's high standards of hygiene. The enemy soldiers tried cats, traps, poisoned grain, water, cheese, even meat, but everything proved to be ineffective, and the rodent population increased to such proportions that from time to time there were rumors that the Commandant was about to order the provisions to be moved elsewhere, and to reopen the school.

SPITTING
OUT
HUNGER

Once in a while I would be drawn by the smell of food and would hang around the fence of the old school building, staring at the guards while they ate their dinner. But even if they had wanted to give me some of the leftovers, the soldiers had strict orders not to, and many times I would return home hungrier than when I left.

One evening, I was so hungry that I found myself unwilling to leave, although the guards had finished eating, and the canteen was closed. The sweet and burning sensation of hunger between my throat and stomach wouldn't go away. I remembered the doctor telling us not to swallow our saliva every time our mouths watered from hunger, because that made the burning even worse. I began to spit. I'd choose targets, aim, and try to direct my spittle at them as accurately as I could. When it got dark, I made an imaginary target with black circles and

tried to hit its center, a round red dot. I had to
concentrate hard in order to keep that target from
moving, but no matter how hard I tried, after a few
minutes the circles started to spin, and the dot became a well of radiant blues, greens, yellows, and
silvers. I got dizzy and held on to the fence, closing
my eyes to wipe out the target, but it kept reappear-
ing within the privacy of my eyelids. I opened my
eyes again, and the target changed to a face that
looked like the Commandant's. I spat at it. I closed
my eyes, opened them, and it changed to the face
of Lekas. I spat at it also. As soon as I did that, it
changed again to become Aunt Liberty's face. I hes-
itated for a moment, but then I spat at it also, and
I spat at my father's face, and my mother's, Uncle
Iasson's, and everybody's face I could think of and
see, including the face of Christ as an infant, His
mother's face, and His father's broad and austere
face done in mosaics, even my own face, and at
each small blinking eye.

A guard opened the gate and let me into the schoolyard. It was late, most of the soldiers had with-
drawn. He led me into a shack where another soldier worked on a big engine, which, as I was told
later, was a generator. The engine made so much
noise that the two men could not hear each other,
and had to communicate with gestures. The mechanic was busy tying a thin copper wire to two
rows of tacks that he'd pinned to the bottom of a
small wooden box. When he finished, the other
handed him a heavy black cube with two pairs of

**THE
MOUSE
CIRCUS**

insulated wires. He connected two of them to the generator, and the other two to the grille in the wooden box. He then asked me to help him by holding the two wires. There was no electricity in our town, and until that day I knew nothing about it, so I went ahead and held the wires as I was told. Immediately, I felt a weak shock, and my fingers grew numb. The two men were amused by my surprise, and rewarded me with a couple of biscuits. I asked, but they refused to explain what had happened. I thought they were testing a new weapon. Then the mechanic left and went into the main school building. The guard lit his pipe. He had a strange grin around his mouth as he smoked, and I worried about what they might be up to. The mechanic returned, bringing a small cage with a mouse in it. He sat on the bench next to me, and, opening the door of the cage, he let the mouse jump out and land on the grille. The mouse was surprised. It squealed and tried to run away. It couldn't. I could hardly imagine how much greater the shock must be to a small creature. The mouse balanced itself on a single wire, panting. The guard and the mechanic were laughing. The mouse looked comical, all right, but gradually I had begun to understand what its funny jumps and squeals meant. I tried to make them stop it, but they didn't pay attention. The little circus fascinated the two men; their faces looked as innocent as children's. The mouse was balancing again on a single wire. When it did that, nothing seemed to happen to it, and it took that opportunity to lick its fur and calm down. But as soon as it stepped on two wires at the same time, it screamed and went crazy, jumping back and forth, not knowing what to do, not knowing where to hide, or from what to hide. Once in a while I could smell burning fur and skin, and twice the mouse was knocked out and lay still. The mechanic took it out of the box and revived it by moving its forelegs up and down, which the guard thought extremely funny, and he laughed loudly, stomping his boots on the floor. But as soon as the mouse stood up again, the mechanic threw it back into the circus. The third round did not last long. Suddenly the mouse seemed to have gotten stuck on the wires. It made a few weak efforts to pull away, but it failed, and, letting out a last squeal, it held still with its mouth half open. There was a small puff of smoke. The mechanic dumped the mouse quickly into a trash can with disgust, before it began to roast.

Next time they let me in, the guard and the mechanic were roasting chestnuts. They picked chestnuts from a charcoal fire that burned in an old helmet, placed them on a shelf to cool down, then shelled them and ate them. A wonderful warm smell filled my nostrils and lungs, making my mouth water. I felt dizzy. I sat on the bench, rubbed my hands over the small fire, and casually stretched a bit further to get a chestnut that seemed to be done. The mechanic hit me on the back of my hand with the tongs, while wagging his index finger to tell me I was not allowed to do that. I showed surprise, but they dismissed my reaction. I stretched my hand toward them. The two men looked at each other, smiling. Then the guard tried to tell me that first I must pull down my pants. I pretended I didn't understand. The guard tried again. I unbuttoned my pants and pulled them down. I saw the mechanic's face change, turn serious. I looked at myself. My skin was covered by large red blotches with swelling tips turning white. I got scared. I began to cry, but that made them

CHESTNUTS
FROM
THE
FIRE

angry. They ordered me to pull up my pants and go home. I buttoned up and opened my hand for a chestnut. The mechanic's finger was wagging again. What now? More gestures: You may have a chestnut on condition that you pick it up with bare fingers, and hold it fast in your fist for as long as it takes to cool before you can eat it. I nodded. I picked a chestnut the shell of which had already caught fire, and closed my fingers around it as tightly as I could. It burned. I concentrated by staring into the mechanic's eyes. They were light gray. I thought of two moist, cool marbles I wouldn't mind playing with. I stared into his eyes without showing any sign of pain from the burn. I knew I could do it without crying, but suddenly my eyes began to water all by themselves. How long did I hold that chestnut in my hand? At some point I thought, It must be cool now, but my hand hurt so much that I couldn't tell. When the pain moved from the skin to the muscle, I was sure that the chestnut was cool enough to eat. Without ceasing to stare at the mechanic, I slowly opened my fingers and let the chestnut drop into the fire. I stood up and silently made for the door. Someone's hand grabbed me on the arm. It was the guard. His face seemed confused, troubled. Had I hurt his feelings? I tried to pull away, but he held me fast, looking at me so seriously that I feared he might even be angry. I stared back at him, and out of the corner of my right eye I saw the mechanic handing me several chestnuts which he had just taken out of the fire. I opened the same hand to receive them, and only then did I realize how badly I was burned. The mechanic shook his head and pointed to my other hand. I shook my head too. I shook my head in a negative motion, and stretched the same hand further toward him.

XI

One afternoon I was out with Flisvos and Philippos looking for food when it started to rain. We ran to Grandmother's for shelter, and I began to go through my shadow theater puppets. Grandmother walked in and said that Dando had been looking for me. "What is this with Dando now?" she asked.

"I don't know. He might be in trouble or something."

I started to talk to Flisvos, to help change the subject, but I could tell she was still thinking about Dando. He was known as the idiot of the town. To me he was just different. A little crazy maybe. And he was also a bastard, found in front of the church in a straw basket. That was long before I was born. Most people said that Dando was born to a woman who was too old to have children, and shouldn't have had children anyway, since she wasn't married. Dando had been adopted by another woman, who'd lost her own child at birth. "Poor Dando," the townspeople used to say when they saw him, or referred to him, and they shook their heads regretfully. "Poor Dando!" And they sighed deeply before changing the subject. That was partly because his second mother had died soon after taking him in,

DANDO

and Dando grew up like a stray puppy, living on scraps. At the age of eight or nine he moved close to the dumps, where he put together a little shack, using a few sheets of corrugated tin and boards that he had salvaged. Some thought he should have been sent to an orphanage or asylum of some sort, but no one really cared enough to follow up that idea. So they let him take care of himself in his own way, and eventually they stopped giving him food, since he seemed old enough to steal. "Poor Dando," sighed Grandmother.

YOU DID WHAT?

I went out into the rain, took a shortcut to the dumps. No, he wasn't an idiot, just different from the others. Poor Dando! His name was all he possessed. But at least it was all his own. Everybody agreed on that. He had never been baptized, never given a proper name like everybody else. According to the priest, he really had no right to go to paradise when his time was up. Dando worried about it. He worried that the name he'd finally given himself was unacceptable in paradise, and worth nothing in hell. He had gone to the priest begging for a name. "Any small crummy name that no one else wants," he had begged, but the priest made it sound impossible: Dando had no birth certificate, no parents, no godparents, and no money. "But let me think about it," said the priest. That's all he said, and Dando took it as a promise of some kind, and to show his appreciation he began to take the priest's cow to the marshes, to feed her in the tall grass. Poor Dando! And the priest was still thinking about it. . . .

I was soaking wet when I got to his shack. The rain made the garbage heaps nearby smell more foul than ever. I knocked hard on his door.

"Who's there?" He sounded scared.

I knocked again and pushed the door open. He

74

was standing in the middle of the small room, shaking. He looked pale, scared. I took off my jacket and dried my hair on its lining. I hadn't been in his place for weeks. Somehow it looked in better shape than the last time I was there. I didn't check, but I had the feeling that he'd stopped using one of the corners of his room as a toilet. The strongest odor I could detect came from a pile of rags that he used to sleep in.

"What's up?" I asked.

Instead of answering, he began to scratch his chin. For the first time I noticed something like a soft blond beard forming around the lower part of his face.

"Say, are you growing a beard?"

He smiled, then his face grew worried again. He began to move around to avoid the drops from the leaking tin roof, and I followed him step by step, asking what was the matter with him. That strange dance around the drops was sort of fun, but I was already wet and I was getting tired of Dando's silence.

"If nothing is the matter, I'll be going back," I said.

"Wait."

"Well?"

"You walked all the raining while here," he finally said.

"That's not the right way to say that."

"Raining all the while?"

"Forget it. Just tell me what's happening."

He closed his eyes as if he were trying to think, but without interrupting the raindrop dance.

"I can't remember," he said and started to cry.

"Try harder," I said.

He stopped, allowing a drop to fall on top of his head. "I'll tell," he mumbled. "I did bad things."

"Like what?"

"Fucked a little cow."

"You did what?"

The second drop that landed on his head made him duck as though he'd been hit by a stone. He wiped his brow, looked at his hand the way one looks at blood, and I thought he would faint.

"How did it happen, Dando?"

"It was the priest's cow."

"I can guess that much. Nobody else in town owns a cow. What I mean is, how did you do it?"

"Oh," he said, "I tied the cow to the wild pear tree, and I hung from a branch so she couldn't kick me."

"I don't believe you."

"There was blood too," said Dando.

"Did you get hurt?"

He shook his head as if to shake the water off his hair.

"Where did the blood come from?"

"The cow."

There was water dripping on our heads constantly, but it didn't seem to matter too much.

"That was a terrible thing to do," I said gravely.

"You don't know nothing," he said shyly, but with conviction, and then he smiled.

"You are going to get yourself into bad trouble, Dando."

His face became worried again. "The monster," he said, shivering.

"You are not a monster. So you shouldn't behave like one."

"The cow will make a monster," he said, "half cow, half man."

"That's right. It happened before."

Dando began to cry.

POOR DANDO

By the time the rain had finally slowed down, it had gotten dark. Dando was feeling better. I put on my jacket, but at that moment we heard a pounding on the tin door, followed immediately by shouts:

"Raise both hands, and come out slowly! Come out one at a time. You are surrounded!"

Dando curled up in his corner, hiding his face in his hands. "It's Lekas," he said, trembling. "They found out."

"Found out what?"

"About the cow."

"Surrender, or we'll huff and puff and blow your tin can in," shouted the man outside the door.

"Don't shoot. I won't do it again," cried Dando.

"Drop your arms, open the door slowly, and surrender!"

This time I recognized Lekas' voice. "Take it easy, we're unarmed," I shouted back.

"They'll kill me. They'll just kill me, I know it," whimpered Dando.

"Don't be stupid. I'll go first," I said. I pulled the door open slowly and raised my hands. Lekas' flashlight hit my face.

"You," he said, surprised. "Where's that bastard?"

Dando came out, crying loudly, "I won't do it again, I swear."

"Shut up, and tell me where the Unnamed One is," said Lekas, directing his beam inside the shack.

"We don't know," I said.

Two more informers armed with rifles and hand grenades closed in from behind the shack.

"He's not in there," said Lekas.

"What are we going to do with these two?" asked one of the others.

Lekas sat on a stone and unwrapped a chocolate bar. He began to lick it thoughtfully. "Shoot them," he said calmly, looking at his chocolate.

I felt something like a snake coiling up tightly in my stomach, and my knees losing their strength. Dando, already on his knees, was crying and stuttering words I could not understand.

"What about scarves for their eyes?" asked one of the informers.

"Come on, don't waste my time," said Lekas,

standing up and pushing the rest of the chocolate into his mouth. "This isn't a formal execution. Shoot them and drag the bodies to the trash heaps."

The informers yanked us up and pushed us against two trees. Dando fell down again. They lifted him up, but once again he collapsed. Then Lekas went and whispered something to them. "Sure," they said.

"Aim," said Lekas.

My Uncle Thanasis' small figure appeared once more, this time climbing the ridges of the corrugated tin wall, picking up fragments of glass and lead. He hadn't shaved for days. He opened his mouth to say something, and I stopped breathing to hear whether or not the voice I'd hear next would be his.

"Fire!"

The snake in my stomach loosened up, and with closed eyes I saw a watermelon cracking, then splitting in two. I fell on my knees, trying to concentrate on a quick succession of images, sensations, thoughts, to find out all about death's touch and takeover. I felt no pain anywhere, and I twitched, hoping to locate my wounds. Nothing. Then I remembered someone saying that the bullet is sweet, doesn't hurt right away, probably because the lead is hot. Somewhere in the distance I heard the informers: "Look, they're still twitching."

"Let's get going," said Lekas. "The dogs will finish them off."

They walked away, whispering to each other and laughing. Then I heard Dando's body heaving in the mud. It sounded as though only part of his body were there, beating the ground, writhing like a lizard's tail, while the rest of him was gone. I thought of turning toward him to look, but I was afraid that all I'd see would be a huge green tail with a scab of mud at the point of severance. Then I felt something warm trickling down my left leg, and all my attention returned to my own body. I twitched again, unwillingly, as the warmth spread to my belly and crotch. Why did it take so long to feel the pain? How long would it take for the lead to cool off? I touched my leg and brought my hand close to my eyes, trying to see the blood. There was not enough light to tell, but the smell was familiar: piss. Slowly, I stood up, determined to find my wounds by running my hands over my body. Suddenly the moon came out, and I saw the bullet hole in the bark of the tree.

"Dando!"

Had they missed? My heart, as if taking advantage of my confusion, was beating violently. No, they couldn't have missed. No, they never meant to kill us with bullets. Only scare us to death. Insane with hope, I rubbed my whole body with my hands, and let out a wild cry, at the end of which I was again frightened. What was it that made Lekas and the other informers do that? I saw the moon rising over the heaps of refuse. Dando was crawling weakly toward the door of the shack.

"Dando!"

"I am dead," he whispered. He stopped and let his face rest on the wet grass.

"No, no, you're alive. Look at the moon!" I felt that the moon was lifting me up, that I was rising above the ground, and that Dando was unwilling to come along.

"I am dead."

I unbuttoned his shirt, searched him. No blood. The moon was bright enough; if Dando had been hit I'd know it. He was pale, but not because of any loss of blood or rupture of a vital organ.

"Look, Dando, there's no blood. The bullet missed you."

"Then how come I'm dead?"

"You're not dead. You can't be dead. You're talking to me."

"You don't know nothing," he said.

His skin was white, and his eyes rolled back in his

head. I dragged him inside, let him rest on the heap of rags he used to sleep in, and I sat by, waiting for him to recover. He remained pale, shivering, talking in his delirium, repeating time and again the word "dead." I sat by, talking to him, waiting for him to recover, and when he quieted down and seemed to be asleep, I covered him with an old coat, and walked home. And when I went back the next morning to see him, I found him dead.

THE REAL FACE OF GOD

Since Dando hadn't been baptized, he did not qualify for a funeral service, and the priest wouldn't even let us bury his body in the cemetery. We took Dando to the hills, we took him and buried him under a pine tree, near the prisoner who according to official records had taken his own life. The same group of people again, except the old teacher, who was sick in bed. Xanthi tried to deliver a eulogy but failed. She talked about idiots, bread thieves, poets, and other people whom nobody, not even God, understood; but when she mentioned the whores, she broke into tears, and the eulogy ended there. Then something unexpected happened. It started with Tryfos.

"Well, that's a treacherous god for you," he shouted, startling everybody. "I'm a peasant, but I can tell you I know more about spies, poets, and whores than God knows. Don't you? Don't you? Don't you?" he said, pointing to others in the crowd. His face was getting red; he was angry.

Everyone turned, staring at him in silence.

"Don't you?" he repeated.

One after another, people began to respond: "Yes."

"That's right."

"That's exactly the way it is."

"Long live Dando's memory!"

Tryfos raised his hands, and when the crowd had quieted down, he spoke again: "The question is, Does God know anything at all? Does He know what in hell is going on down here?"

"I doubt it," said somebody.

"Chances are He doesn't know, and He doesn't give a damn," said another.

"That's what I'm afraid of," sighed Tryfos, "and that's why this time I'm not going to throw a handful of dirt into the grave. What I am going to do is throw a handful of dirt into His face."

"Yes! Yes!" shouted several people at once.

"Long live Dando!"

"Long live the whores!"

I saw an old couple crossing themselves in fear and starting to leave. But the rest of us took handfuls of dirt and aimed high. We aimed at His face, His broad, indifferent face as we knew it from the ikons, His eyes twinkling like morning stars, His lips moist.

"Come on," said Philippos, and Flisvos said, "Where?" "There," said Philippos, casting his handful in the air like the others, but all that dirt kept coming back to us, kept falling on our faces and hair. The dirt wouldn't stick to God's face, His face was deceptively distant. Once again He seemed to have the upper hand. "He's nowhere," said Flisvos, but I did not agree with him. "He's over there," I said, "here and there, in everything, in every one of us. Isn't that what they say?" And having said that, I took another fistful of dirt and hit Flisvos in the face. It seemed to make sense, because he recovered quickly. I stood still. I stood, and he hit me as hard; and then Philippos and the others, seeing the real face of God, began to swing their fistfuls at one another, and by the time we had exhausted ourselves, the real face of God was again familiar.

XII

"Listen."

I heard the whistle, turned, and saw the black smoke of the coal engine leaping over houses and naked trees.

"The train."

The enemy soldier in charge of the station lowered the stop flag and pushed the crowd clear of the tracks.

"Why is it going so slowly?"

"It's pushing a cage."

The setting sun spread a pure tangerine glow over the western sky, warming the bare landscape. A hawk made a broad circle, then hovered for a few moments and, stretching its neck downward, remained transfixed, as if scanning the ground; and the ground underneath rose steadily until the hawk's talons touched down. When the train appeared in the distance, the mountains receded into a violet haze.

"The cage, the cage."

Since the Mountain Fighters had begun to blow up supply trains, the enemy always attached a car full of hostages to the front of the engine. These prison cars were specially made cages with steel bars, like the ones used for wild animals in a circus, but the traveling hostages had no destination, they were part of the train, clearing the way for the rest of the train, knowing that their only chance to be cut loose from the train would come when the cage ran into a mine, a mine buried under the tracks by Mountain Fighters.

"The cage."

The train came to a halt, and several enemy soldiers began to unload cases of ammunition and other cargo. We gathered around the cage, looking at the hostages, hoping to recognize a relative or a familiar face among them. The hostages, some fifty or sixty of them, mostly old people and children, looked searchingly at us. They were pale, exhausted from the endless ride. They'd been exposed to the sun, the rain, and the wind, then to the sun again. Their hair, their skin, and their clothes were covered with dust and soot. It took less than a minute for everybody to look at everybody, but none could relinquish hope. One more time around. Did I miss one? Did someone miss me? But the more we stared at each other, the more familiar we seemed to each other. Some closed their eyes, some turned their faces the other way, others began to touch, stretch out hands, force faces between two bars, then close their eyes and kiss before turning their faces the other way. The train whistled. A kid inside the cage showed me his arm; he wore a band with a big yellow star on it. He must have been a general in his neighborhood army when he played war with the other kids—a great general. That's why the enemy grabbed him. I stood at attention, acknowledging his rank, and saluted him. Then Flisvos and Philippos saluted him also, and as the train began to slide past, exhaling slow, violent puffs of smoke, the kid with the yellow star in the cage smiled and returned the salute.

ARSON   On my way back home, I found our block surrounded by enemy soldiers, informers, and dogs.

"Get back! Get back, or you'll get it between the
eyes!"

"Relax, I'm unarmed," I shouted back.

I heard several men laugh, and I recognized
Lekas' voice: "Put your hands up high, and approach slowly!"

"He's the old witch's grandson," explained another informer.

Someone fixed a flashlight beam on my face.
When I got close, I saw the Commandant dressed
in a field uniform, whispering something in Lekas'
ear. The chief informer pushed me forward, and
followed me home.

"This is my neighborhood," I said. "I know my
way."

"Shut up, and keep on moving," said Lekas,
pushing me with the butt of his rifle.

"If you're looking for someone young and mean
around here, you're wasting your time," I said.

"The devil with him," grunted Lekas.

When we got home, he motioned to me to knock
on the door.

Grandma: "If you are the Unnamed One, go
away. This house is guarded by the Virgin, who's
my namesake!"

Me: "Grandma, open up. The Virgin might be
guarding the house, but wait until you see all the
angels around the neighborhood."

Lekas: "Shut up, I'm telling you!"

Grandma: "I see now. You just wait a minute
until I can find the key, my boy."

What key? The key was always in the keyhole. It
took Grandmother quite a bit of time to get back,
and even more time to unlock the door. I could tell

she'd gotten the message and was stalling. When she finally opened up, I saw a strange red glow on the wall behind her. I wondered what she was up to.

"Good evening, Aunt," said Lekas, noticing the glow, which kept growing larger inside the house. "I'm sorry, but I have orders to search the house," he added awkwardly.

"I'm equally sorry, but you can't come in," said Grandmother.

Lekas stiffened up: "I said I have orders—"

"You just can't come in," she repeated firmly.

"Why?" Lekas was losing his patience.

"Because the house is burning, that's why!" she answered triumphantly, and right at that moment, big red flames leaped upward to the window curtains and the ceiling, and within minutes the entire house was on fire.

"That's how my first collection of shadow theater puppets finally perished," I remembered Phlox saying, while wiping his eyes with the back of his hand. "How?" I had asked, trying to catch up with the story, the beginning of which I had missed. "You know the story of the heroic monk who was burned alive at the stake, right? Well, I had this idea, you see, instead of using a sheet of transparent paper to imitate the fire behind the screen, to actually light a fire and burn the paper puppet of the monk, for the whole thing to look more real." "And then what?" I'd asked. "First the cheesecloth screen caught fire. Then the boards of the stage and the plywood sky, then the rest of the puppets. They all went up in flames like the monk. The best, the most expensive ones, had been made of cow and camel hide. Beautiful, beautiful pieces. I tried to save some of them, but all I managed to do was burn my hands. First the puppets, then my own hands."

FIRE
AND
PHLOX

RESCUE   Soldiers, informers, and a few neighbors were
standing by in the street, watching our house burn.
As I rushed out the door holding the basket with my
own shadow theater puppets, I saw the reflection of
the flames on the faces of the crowd. Their mouths
opened as in a chorus, but I didn't hear their voices.
When I opened my eyes again, I saw I was naked.
Grandmother had stripped my smoking clothes off,
and another woman was rubbing my back with a
wet towel. At that moment, the roof of the house
caved in with a great noise, and I looked around for
my puppets.

"Here they are, don't worry," said my grandmother, handing me the full basket.

Later on I asked Grandmother if the Unnamed
One had really been hiding in our house that night.

"Of course not," she said. "Would I burn the
house down if he were hiding in it?"

"I guess not. But then why did you burn it down?"

"To save him," she said, and the gold tooth rose
in the dark of her mouth like a small moon. "You
figure it out," she added. She wouldn't burn down
the house if he were in it, and that made sense.

"But how could you save him by burning the
house if he wasn't in it?"

"Figure it out," she said.

"Grandma, where are we going to spend the winter with no house now?"

"Come winter, we'll think of something."

Several days later Grandmother told me that the
Unnamed One was in fact hiding in a nearby house
when the enemy blocked the neighborhood. By setting fire to our house, she distracted the enemy,
and made it possible for Mikés to escape. "Don't
feel bad about it," she chuckled. "The enemy hasn't
figured it out either."

86

XIII

" 'When the devil has no work to do, he screws his own children,' says an old proverb; but this one devil, poor devil, was childless . . ." Old Petros paused to roll a cigarette in a cornhusk, and looked around at each one of us, stopping at me. "This one's too young for my stories," he said.

A
TALE
TOLD
IN
TWO
PARTS

"Beat it," said my cousin Aris. "Go home."

I got up, took a few steps backward, and sat down again. Old Petros was a fisherman from a neighboring town. He had a reputation for knowing a lot of spicy stories, which he'd tell only in installments. He lit his cigarette, and then blew the smoke back at it thoughtfully.

". . . but this one devil was childless, so he kept screwing himself by smoking horse shit wrapped in cornhusks," he said self-mockingly. There were a few laughs, but the gathering was getting impatient for the real story. "All right, all right," he said, raising his hands. "He was childless, so he kept screwing other people's children— Yes, I mean it. He used to hang around a boys' boarding school, and when he saw a nice-looking one with red cheeks, he'd offer to take him on a boat ride around the bay. Now if the boy accepted, the fisherman would soon take him by a large rock that stood right in the entry of the bay. There were several fig trees growing on it, so the boy almost always welcomed his host's suggestion to stop and pick a few figs, and in the cool shade of the fig trees the old rascal had the time of his life." Once more there were a few laughs.

"Come on, that's not all, is it?" said Tryfos, who was one of the listeners.

"No, I guess not. That would be too short, wouldn't it?"

"That's right."

"Let me see now . . . Ah, yes. Well, the years went by, and the fisherman couldn't help but notice that one after another the boys he'd once screwed were making brilliant careers: generals, businessmen, doctors, lawyers, mayors. There was even one who became a prime minister. And then the fisherman realized that he himself was getting poorer and poorer. There's something wrong somewhere, he thought. Suppose I am the luckiest guy on earth, and all I have been doing is wasting my good luck on others. . . . Hell, better late than never, he thought, and got into his boat and sailed to the rock, alone this time. That was about five in the afternoon. Just then, the Governor showed up on the balcony of his office overlooking the bay for his afternoon coffee and snack of fresh figs. When he saw the boat docking at the rock and the fisherman getting out, he asked for his spyglass. From that moment on, until the old man got back to his boat and sailed to the mole, the Governor observed his every movement, and at the end he ordered two Coast Guard officers to go and bring the fisherman before him."

Old Petros took a deep breath, then looked around at his audience with satisfaction. "I got to get going now," he said, preparing himself to stand up.

A dozen hands laid hold of him by the head, the

shoulders, and the arms, forcing him to sit still.

"Come on, you know the rules," he protested. "You'll have to wait for the conclusion until my next visit. In the meantime you can try and guess what the old fucker did all by himself on that rock, and what the Governor, who saw everything through the spyglass, had in mind."

They wouldn't let go of him.

"I mean it," he protested again. "I just don't have the rest of it yet."

"I have something else that might interest you, though," continued Old Petros, "except this one's neither funny nor dirty. It's plain ordinary history. Are you interested in plain ordinary history?"

"No," shouted Tryfos.

"It depends," said Kyr Notis the grocer.

"What's plain ordinary history, anyway?" asked Aris.

"Numbers," replied Old Petros; "numbers and episodes."

"Anything that's neither funny nor dirty can be pretty boring," brooded Tryfos.

"You might have a point there," said Old Petros. "So don't blame me if that's how these first episodes from the true story of R. strike you."

"Who's R.?" asked Kyr Notis.

"Listen and you might figure it out," said Old Petros. And he told this story:

AGENT R.
(1–7)

1. Besides those who took to the mountain when

the enemy invaded our country, there were others who sailed with their families across the sea to T., then a neutral country.

2. R. said their final destination was E., where the Allied Command had its headquarters. Their plan called for the women and children to live in relative safety, and for the men to join the war effort from there.

3. While crossing T. by foot, the refugees were attacked, robbed, raped, and then shot by bandits and gendarmes alike. R. was the only one to survive. In spite of a bullet wound in his shoulder, he buried his wife and child and continued to travel through deserts and mountains toward E.

4. When R. reached E., the Allies put him through a crash training program for special operations. The training completed, R. was sent on a secret mission back to our country with money for messengers and with explosives, a field radio, and a radio operator who knew languages.

5. They arrived on the mountain and settled in a cave to work at their task. The first night, the radio operator tried to kill R. and steal the money. R., who had excellent training, disarmed him and put him back to work.

6. A message came through the radio from the Allied Command instructing R. to cooperate with the Mountain Fighters. R. carried out the directive. He worked mostly with Capetan Perseus, who was

suspicious of the Allies. It wasn't easy for R. to work with Capetan Perseus, God rest his soul, and at the same time keep an eye on the radio operator.

7. When their tasks were accomplished, R. and the radio operator found their way to the coast, where they were picked up by an Allied submarine, heading for . . .

"Say, where's everybody going?" said Old Petros, interrupting himself. "I haven't finished it yet. Isn't anyone interested in plain ordinary history anymore?"

XIV

ARIS'
DILEMMA

Aris was secretly in love with Lemonia, the priest's older daughter, but she didn't seem to notice. Aris was discouraged. He was so discouraged that he decided to join the Mountain Fighters. He talked about it to his parents. He said it was a shame for him to be wasting away like that while others risked everything for freedom. His father thought that was an interesting way to put it, but his mother, my aunt, was less sure. Although she preferred almost anything to Aris' getting married, she said that if he joined the Mountain Fighters he'd probably get killed or captured and tortured to death, because his eyesight was so poor that he could hardly tell a baker from a beggar.

THE
DECIDED
ONE

When winter came, Grandmother and I moved to the family house of Mikés, which had been boarded up since Aunt Liberty's death. Mikés, who was still at large, would visit once in a while to spend the night and share with us whatever we or he could provide. The first few times I saw him, I was so excited that I had a hard time keeping it from Flisvos and Philippos. But the more I saw of him, the more confused I felt about heroic legends. His obsession with revenge, which excited the imagination of the townspeople, disturbed me more than fascinated me. I couldn't see much of a connection between revenge and our struggle for survival. On the contrary, revenge was something worth fighting against if we were to survive. Didn't Mikés know that?

"I don't know anyone by the name of Mikés," said Grandmother.

"You mean to say the Unnamed One," said Aris.

"Yes, the Unnamed One."

"Now, what was the question?" asked Grandmother.

Mikés was sixteen. He was no longer a youngster, and not yet an adult. He was a "decided one," one who had been marked for death prematurely, so the exact number of his years was not important, the moment of his death was. Can't you see, Grandmother?

"If he is marked, he is marked. But they're marked too," she said. "He has a red cross on his brow, but they have a red line around their necks. It takes a knife and a steady hand, that's all it takes," she said.

Mikés was skinny and pale, with hazel eyes and straight brown hair. His lips were thin and moved only slightly when he spoke. When he spoke, he often changed the subject, usually at a crucial point, as if he were unable to find the right words to continue. Grandmother cared for him with a passion that made me jealous. Still, I never heard her give him a word of caution. Even when he brought home a heavy Steyr submachine gun, Grandmother seemed to be more excited and proud of him than alarmed.

He was young enough to be my brother, and old enough to be the Devil himself. But devils and angels alike were in the service of Death. We were surrounded by death, and the only way out was dying. The fact of death, following the confusion about the idea of death. So much so that to survive was often an accident. "One's got to do what he's marked for," Grandmother would say when I'd ask her why she didn't advise the Unnamed One to forget the revenge and stay alive. And when I asked him that myself, his answer was "My life doesn't count; theirs does. So it's their death that's important, not mine."

As the first anniversary of his brother's death drew near, Mikés' visits became rare and short. When he was with us, he just sat in a chair, staring silently at his Steyr, which he held in his lap like a lifeless child. One evening he asked Grandmother to heat water so he could wash his hair and his body, which had started to smell. He said so without looking at Grandmother. He washed, changed to clean underwear, then took a pair of scissors and clipped his hair as short as he could. Grandmother and I watched without questioning. Later on he took out pencil and paper and drew a little map. He marked the map and studied it for some time, silently. I went to bed and woke up just before dawn, when Grandmother lit the lamp. Mikés was standing in the middle of the room, dressed in what must have been his Sunday suit a year before. Somewhat smaller than his size, and wrinkled. He had assumed a kind of formal posture, a strange, comical look, but his white shirt unbuttoned at the top seemed nice on him, and made him look handsome.

Old smells, in old, very old drawers, closets, and trunks that haven't been opened for years—you'd think there'd be nothing in them any longer but smell, the smell of trapped air, the memory of clothes worn years ago, the breaths of people now dead and forgotten. Have you and I seen them before? When was it? And where? And why does it seem to matter? Mikés compares the palms of his hands with one another as though there ought to be significance in their nearly perfect resemblance, and then, all of a sudden, there is a terrible weapon between his hands.

Mikés washed his body, clipped his hair, wore his Sunday clothes, tied a black-black band around his forehead, knelt in front of Grandmother, kissed her hand, kissed me on both my cheeks, ruffled my hair, lifted an empty bottle to his lips, drank, touched the earth in the dark, pricked the tip of his finger to watch his blood—"Good flow," he said— hid his weapon in his coat under his arm—how heavy—slipped out softly like a cat, hurry now before the light of dawn slips out before you get there, his brother's anniversary and his own when.

I hid my face in Grandmother's apron, she snuffed out the light. A barrage, a barrage, one-two minutes—or was it seconds? A barrage, a barrage. We take turns to wake from this kind of dream, but sleep overtakes us again, and my lips twitch as a bony angel casts his shadow over my bed before kissing me, and he's unable to tell, and unnamable, his name could be Michael, he could be anybody.

"Mikés sacked the Security Station! The Devil took revenge! He kicked the door in and gunned down everyone there, including the murderers of his brother and mother, and another informer who had been there questioning a prisoner all night."

"What about himself—did he get away?"

"I wish that neighbor of yours, that Lekas, had been there to get all the buttonholes he deserves."

"But what about Mikés himself?"

"Listen, he finished off five of them. That's out of five who were there. He even set fire to the security files."

"What happened then?"

"He made for the basement to release the prisoner, but one of the soldiers who lay on the floor dying drew his pistol and shot him in the back."

XV

Lekas was a widower. Grandmother once said that he'd killed his wife by beating her. Now there were rumors that he lived with a red-haired woman from another town. Lekas had never known hunger. His back yard had many fruit trees, something for every season, but only he, a few enemy officers, and the fruit flies enjoyed them. The stone wall around the yard was high and had a roofing of mortar with fragments of glass built in, so that no one from the outside could climb over it. And he was so afraid of possible attempts on his life that he was ready to shoot at anything that moved in that back yard at night. Then Uncle Iasson said that Lekas was so jealous of the red-haired woman that he never allowed her to go out, even to go to church. And he said, "All day long she has to stay in, with no one to talk to, so all day long she washes her body and brushes her hair and puts on lipstick and perfume in front of the mirror, waiting for Lekas to come home."

Grandfather warned Uncle Iasson to keep away from Lekas' house.

LEKAS'
SECRETS

THE
POET
One day I found Uncle Iasson reading an old hand-written book of poems and stories. "Here, listen to this one," he said, and began to read aloud:

". . . the forest of your lungs, the thickets of your glands, the flutes, the sexual expansion of your marrow. The vacuum in your joints, and your many mineral springs. And the dark dome of your skull where stars blossom and fall silently. Throw a little coin skyward; even the most distant spectator will hear its impact. The root, the trunk, the branches, the leaves, the bloom, the fruit, and the seed—the root. You are a tree, and the forest will never be the same again without you. Look at the course and the formation of the clouds beneath your fingernails. It's those clouds that change the landscape when you point at it. The clouds, and the rain that follows. Wash your thought in sea water, then wash away the salt. Your sweating back glistens as you bend to lift the stones and the logs—are you building a shelter?—and your spine is the ridge of the mountain. Symmetry and sensation, however ephemeral. Just don't forget the shelter for the birds on the roof of your shelter. Don't let the gap in the rock ever depress you; the gap will soon fill with flowers. And don't let the gap in the sea postpone your voyage; the sea will throw aside her arms for the sea to pass, and the most distant spectator will envy your fortune."

"Well, what do you think?" said Uncle Iasson.
"It sounds nice, but I don't get it."
"I don't get it either, but I like it," said Uncle Iasson.
"Didn't you write it yourself?" I asked.
"No, I didn't."
Uncle Iasson said that the whole book had been

98

written by a poet who had died young, long before
the war. His name was Alexis, he said. He was the
son of the old blind singer who still lives, but Alexis
was different. When he spoke, only a few could
really tell what he was talking about, and when he
refused to say anything for weeks, even fewer
understood why. He was a really strange character,
said Uncle Iasson.

"But how do you know all this?" I asked.

"Uncle Spanos told me," said Uncle Iasson. "It
was he who gave me the book, to begin with." Then
Uncle Iasson promised to let me read that book too,
once he was through.

In the meantime, I went to see Uncle Spanos,
hoping to learn more about Alexis the poet.

"He wore a cape, black cape on his bony shoulders," said Uncle Spanos, "and his hair was long
and flowing in the wind like a woman's. In fact, no
one could tell if he were a man or a woman for sure.
He drove a chariot around town—of all the crazy
things!" said Uncle Spanos. And he said, "He had
it specially made, of course. He gave the carpenters
a hard time, but finally they came up with one.
'Hell, it's not quite what I had in mind, but it will
do for now,' the poet said. To tell the truth, it
turned out to be a beautiful chariot—sturdy and
colorful like the ones our ancestors used in the old
time," said Uncle Spanos. "But one fine Sunday
morning, when everyone else went to church, Alexis raced through the square with his two black
horses and his chariot, and we thought it was the
Prophet Elias coming to pass judgment on the sinners, except he drove all the way to the end of the
town and over the cliffs into the deep sea."

"Why?"

"No one knows. People had to make up all kinds
of stories to explain Alexis' strange life and death,
and the old singer, his father, made a lot of songs
about him, the way he still does about others, but I
doubt that he really knew his son. Then our priest

excommunicated Alexis, shouting three times, 'Anathema,' just in case he still lived. . . . But what the sea takes, the sea won't give back," sighed Uncle Spanos, throwing a handful of pebbles into the water. "See the concrete ships? The enemy built them specially to store munitions out of the reach of the Mountain Fighters, but one of these days the sea will shiver, and growl, and rise, and roll forth, and the concrete ships will be no more. And then we'll take the boats out there, and spread the nets again."

THE
SEA
AND
THE
RIVER

"Uncle Spanos, what was it like in the old days?"

"We used to take the nets out in two boats and spread them crescent-like, then bring the lines back to the shore. Five in the morning, the two teams would drag the nets a foot at a time to the Captain's order: Eeeeop! Eeeeop! In an hour's time or so, the sack would be brought out, loaded with fish that leaped in the air, slippery, silver. We'd divide the catch and take it to the streets. Broad, shallow baskets on top of our heads—first to the restaurants and the tavernas, then to the neighborhoods. The basket makes a fine shade in the summer, protects you from the sun, but as the day wears out, the fish smell gets stronger, so we'd be glad to have sold out by noon. Later in the day, we repaired the nets, replaced the lead and cork that was lost, put things in order for the night, got some rest. Our skin was tanned, cured by the salt and the sea wind. No one else's skin shone like ours. Walking out of the boats at daybreak, our arms and legs sparkling with the fish scales, we looked as if we were turning into fishes ourselves. But now the enemy has jammed the bay with concrete ships, ships made for oil and munitions storage. See that garland of red cans floating all around? Underneath each one of them is a sea mine to keep out the submarines. And you can see the cannons on top of the concrete turrets. Those are to protect the enemy against air attacks. So, my boy, the Lord multiplies the fish, but the enemy won't let us catch them. The enemy, you know, has always been a meat eater," said Uncle Spanos, throwing a handful of pebbles into the water.

We then walked over to the river, hoping to catch a few eels. Slow river, stinkweed, water snakes, and toads. Burn a branch of stinkweed, and stir the water with it. That makes the eels dizzy, makes them lose their sense of direction. They just relax and drift downstream right into your basket and coil there, happy to have found a nice round place to rest. So do water snakes.

"Not true," said Uncle Spanos.

"But how can you tell the difference between water snakes and eels?"

"Don't worry about water snakes. Just watch out for leeches."

"Too late, Uncle Spanos."

XVI

MOSAICS   Since the enemy had brought in the concrete ships and mined the bay, fishing was forbidden, and many people were afraid even to go swimming. Flisvos would go to the beach only to collect colored stones; my cousin Philippos would join him, but mostly to look for soft-shelled crabs under the rocks, which he ate raw. And I went along, making mosaics. I would spend a couple of hours at a time composing a sailboat with red and white pebbles on a smooth bed of sand, but then Flisvos would find a colored stone with a ready-made picture of the same boat on it. We'd start an argument about which picture was more interesting and would call Philippos to give an impartial opinion. He'd stand by, compare, then put his hand on Flisvos' shoulder and say, "You've done it again." Turning to me, he'd remark, "You've got to have the eye, you know." I'd lean back, watching the afternoon tide dismantle my boat, pebble by pebble, and sink it, a perfect wreck. I knew that my mosaics were better than the ready-made pictures Flisvos found on stones, but I couldn't prove it. As time went by, my mosaics grew larger, more colorful, and more time-consuming. The others, tired of waiting for me to finish, would go home without me, and my picture would be swept away by the tide, unappreciated. One day I started early in the morning, and by noon I had finished a mosaic showing Angelica, the priest's second daughter, as a mermaid. I used sparkling white pebbles for the upper part of her body and marbled silvery ones for her tail. Black pebbles for her eyebrows and lashes, and for her hair waving in the wind. The pupils of her eyes were dark green. Her lips and nipples were pale pink, for which I could find no pebbles and had to crush an old ceramic tile to get them right. Blue wavy lines crested with rows of white pebbles across the lower part of the picture made the water transparent and Angelica's fishtail submerged and visible. In one hand she held a tiny boat with a white sail, and in the other a flaming little heart. By the time I finished the picture, I was in love with Angelica. I sat down wondering about it while waiting for Flisvos and Philippos. Sure, I had always liked Angelica—everybody else did too, in spite of her father the priest, who had a bad temper and was an enemy sympathizer—but until I finished that mosaic, I hadn't had any special feelings for her. Now I wished that Flisvos and Philippos would never come to pass judgment on her. I wished only that she would come to see and admire herself and her maker. . . .

Flisvos spent the rest of the day combing the beach, unable to find Angelica on a single stone, and Philippos conceded that my mosaic was the damnedest sexiest thing he'd ever seen. During the next few days, they busied themselves with spreading the word about the mosaic depicting Angelica as a mermaid, and I knew that my excommunication was only a matter of time.

Uncle Iasson said, "You are too young for this kind of thing."

Grandmother said, "You are too young for her."

IKONS

Grandfather said, "She's pretty, but she doesn't have it."

"It?"

"Red hair."

Aunt Zoë said, "A romance at this age can only cause grief."

Uncle Spanos said, "That's right, a mermaid can only flap her tail at you."

Aris, who was in love with Angelica's older sister, said, "So that's why you're getting thinner and thinner."

Kyr Notis the grocer said, "I heard the priest is looking for you."

The priest found me, he pulled my ear, told me to start making mosaics of saints, or else . . . And to start going to church on Sundays, or else . . . And to fast for my sinful mind, or else . . . I had been fasting like everybody else, for months, unwillingly. "That's not enough; unwillingly doesn't count," he said. "Sunday, you'll come to the church, or else . . ." I thought about it. For one thing, Angelica would be there.

"What do you think, Grandma?"

Grandmother thought love had shaken up my mind completely. Then she gave me a strange look, and went about washing, patching, and pressing my pants and shirt for the Liturgy.

I entered the church like a lost and found sheep. Shy, self-conscious, I walked straight forward with my hands crossed, and stood with the other kids my age, in the front on the right side. The girls were standing on the left. I couldn't turn to look for Angelica, but she, together with everybody else, surely was staring at me.

The priest came out to read the gospel, and gave me a piercing look. To avoid his eyes, I began to study the ikons: IC.XC., Mary, the Trinity, St. George killing the dragon, St. Demetrios on another horse stabbing a tyrant, the Prophet Elias driving his chariot over mountaintops and clouds. And at the left end of the screen, painted right on the door, the Archangel Michael, with a young face, outspread wings, carrying a flaming sword. Long dark hair waving in the wind, and fine eyebrows, his eyes big like two green almonds, a rather melancholic expression. I wondered at that expression, and I wondered whether or not the monk on the Promontory who'd painted those eyes was falling in love with the Archangel.

At the end of the service, Angelica, who was leaving with her older sister, Lemonia, ahead of me, suddenly turned her face toward me and smiled.

Two o'clock on a hot summer day, dust and desertion. No shade, no wind, the hour the northern enemy becomes homesick—we told you so: This land is arid, doesn't want even us. It has no trees, only an illusion of trees. Like this eucalyptus, so thick, and yet so thirsty that it drinks its own shade—a vast transparency. This is the hour the eucalyptus seeds burst open, tiny yellow puffs, and they fill your breath with pollen, they lure the summer insects away from the houses. Thousands of insects: spiders, flies, mosquitoes, hornets, wasps; spinning, buzzing, crawling all over the tree, licking the pollen, mating, killing for food. This may very well be the last singing tree. Is someone nearby about to die? Is someone else about to return from the dead? Across the street, the priest's house, two stories tall, surrounded by a small flower garden, surrounded by a stone wall that's saddled with broken glass to discourage flower thieves. Blue shutters, blue, blue shutters receding into white walls, and within the house a white peace, and a single fly buzzing occasionally. If it were not for that fly, Angelica wouldn't know how quiet it is; she wouldn't dream, she wouldn't turn in her sleep, she wouldn't

ANGELICA

sigh and struggle with the white sheets on her bed, and her older sister, whose name is not a Christian name, wouldn't ask something, of which Angelica heard only the word "dear." There's always a fly in a quiet cool room at noontime so your midday sleep won't be too deep. In two or three hours from now, a shutter will open with a small white arm following it, the outward motion, the quick withdrawal. She'll go to the garden to draw water, a little water from the well, and her older sister with the pagan name will pour a thin twisting column of water for her to wash arms and face, the last drop hanging from the pitcher's spout like the word "dear."

MOSQUITO BITES

Aris could not believe that Lemonia had no idea about his feelings for her. "If I know about it, she knows it too," he said.

"Even if you haven't had a chance to tell her?"

"Even so."

"How's that supposed to work?"

"Mosquito bites."

"What?"

"It all starts with a mosquito bite, but in fact it takes two—You've heard that expression."

"Yes, but—"

"It comes from the fact that it takes two mosquito bites. First the mosquito goes to the woman and sucks a little bit of her blood. Then it bites the man, leaving a drop of the woman's blood in him."

"So both of them get malaria."

"That too," said Aris, "but I'm talking about something else now. Anyway, as soon as the mosquito leaves a drop of the woman's blood in a man, they both know, and both want more."

"More bites?"

"More blood mixing."

It made sense. The day before I made the mosaic showing Angelica as a mermaid, I'd awakened with a big red spot on my left arm—no doubt a mosquito bite. "Yes, but what happens when all kinds of insects bite and mix the blood of all kinds of people? And why do most people not like mosquitoes and try to kill them?"

"I'll answer your second question first," said Aris. "Most people can't afford to fall in love all the time. Falling in love, like getting malaria, is a damned dangerous thing."

"I see. But what happens when the mosquito bites a man right after having bitten another man? Or an old ugly woman? Or a relative?"

"What can I tell you?" said Aris. "People can't help it. They fall in love just the same."

After having considered the possibilities, I felt grateful that a mosquito had mixed my blood with Angelica's rather than anyone else's.

"I can't tell you how glad I am to know that a mosquito has mixed Lemonia's blood with mine," sighed Aris. "Still, there's a lot of grief in it."

The matchmaker found the priest in a good mood, which was a rare thing, and she took it as a good sign, since there could be no mistake about the purpose of her visit. Lemonia excused herself in order to make coffee, and the old woman took off her scarf and fanned her face with it, making a comment about the heat wave. The priest too thought it unseasonably hot for June, and briefly related that to untimeliness in birth and marriage. The matchmaker listened, and showed neither agreement nor disagreement. But before the priest had a chance to

THE MATCHMAKER

elaborate or even move on to another subject, she said that whenever unusual circumstances prevailed, such as the war, she couldn't help noticing how our everyday life was affected, and she wondered if that too weren't a natural thing.

"In any case, it's a distressing thing," said the priest hastily.

Lemonia walked in, carrying a tray with two cups of coffee, a bowl of candied lemon flowers, and two glasses of water.

"Now, that was perfect timing, my dear," said the matchmaker. "We may drink to you again at your wedding."

"Yes, yes, of course," muttered the priest, clearing his throat.

"Ah, where is your good mother to see you grow so kind and pretty?" went on the matchmaker. "By the way, how old are you, my daughter?"

"Sixteen," said Lemonia, blushing.

"You may be lucky your whole life, and you may live to be a hundred; it's my wish for you."

When Lemonia closed the door behind her, the priest put his hand on the old woman's shoulder. "Let's get to the subject now, woman. Who is it? Who is sending you?"

"Aris," she said in a low tone of voice. "He loves and respects your daughter. As you know, he comes from a good family. Not a rich family, but a very good one."

"Too soon," said the priest, "too soon for him, much too soon for Lemonia. They are just not ready for marriage yet."

"You sound very categorical, Father," said the matchmaker. "I hope you are not doing your own child's future an injustice."

"To tell the truth, I really don't think that Lemonia and Aris were made for each other."

"Don't bet your life on it, Father."

The priest took a spoonful of candy and emptied

it into his mouth thoughtfully. "Does Lemonia know about his feelings?" he asked while still chewing.

"I am not in a position to tell." There seemed to be something like a smile around her wrinkled mouth.

"Lemonia!"

Lemonia walked in so quickly that the old woman knew she had been standing behind the door. The matchmaker, with a gentle motion of her hand, stopped the priest, who was about to address his daughter. "Calm yourself, Father," she said, then turned to Lemonia: "This news is to rejoice over, my dear—if it's news at all—not to be upset about. Aris is an honest, hard-working young man, and with his family's consent I am here to convey his special feelings and respect for you, and to ask how you and your father feel about the possibility of marriage, following a formal engagement, of course, and a period of eight to twelve months."

Lemonia leaned against the doorframe, blushing, then looked at her father.

"I say no," he warned.

Lemonia lowered her eyes to the floor. "I have nothing to say to you," she said to the old woman, and walked out.

The following Sunday, Angelica didn't go to church. Lemonia was accompanied by Chryssa, a friend of hers. I became impatient and left before the end of the service. An hour or so later, Aris came over to see Grandmother, and to tell her that Chryssa had given him a message from Lemonia.

"A good message," he said, "but that old goat the priest is still against it."

"What does Angelica think about all this?" I asked.

"I bet you wondered why she didn't show up

today," he said. And he said, "The answer is, she's ill. There's something wrong with her, and the doctor advised the priest to send her to the Pine Forest for a month or two."

I followed Aris to the door. "When is she leaving?" I asked.

"Soon. And it's a shame, because Lemonia will have to go with her." Aris went out, and in a little while I saw him taking the path to the shore, whistling.

I went out too, and followed him at a distance. When he turned around and saw me, I slowed down.

"Don't you have anything else to do?" he shouted at me. "Go play with Flisvos and Philippos."

I waited for a while, then followed him again all the way to the sea. There I saw him joining a small group of people with Old Petros the storyteller, and I hurried to catch up.

"Now, what do you want to hear this time?" asked Old Petros, rubbing his unshaven chin.

"The rest of it," urged everybody.

"Ah, yes, the rest of it. . . . But which story was it? Where did I stop?"

"Where the Coast Guard officers went to bring the old fucker before the Governor," said Tryfos.

"No, that's the wrong story. That's not where I stopped," said Old Petros.

"What do you mean, the wrong story? You are not going to continue that stupid story of R. first, are you?"

"First the story of R., then the conclusion of the old fucker."

"Oh, no," resounded the chorus.

"Why are you doing this to us?" complained Kyr Notis.

"Because I've just got more news about R., and because I know that a little plain ordinary history won't hurt anyone."

"How about saving that for later," said Tryfos.

"So that you can walk out on me again, right? Oh, no, not again," said Old Petros. And he said, "Now, where was I? Ah, yes, paragraph eight." And he continued:

8. When R. returned to E., the Allied Command refused to pay him his wages, explaining that the radio operator's grievances against him were a serious matter. In addition, R. was given a warning against further transgressions.

AGENT R. (8–15)

9. In addition, he was transferred to the Allied Black Market Squad, which, as R. soon found out, was itself engaged in large-scale marketeering of Allied goods and wholesale transit of hashish.

10. When R. refused to carry out the orders of his superiors in the Black Market Squad, he was arrested and court-martialed. The court proceedings were brief. R. received a suspended sentence of death by hanging, and was sent off on another dangerous mission in enemy-occupied territory.

11. R. arrived in our region and began to gather information about enemy supply ships in the bay, troop movements, trains, and minefields.

12. Although R. had not renewed his contact with the Mountain Fighters, Capetan Andromache tipped him off that the Allies had let the enemy know about his arrival and hiding place.

13. R. didn't believe Capetan Andromache, but he moved to another hiding place, just in case.

14. Next day, enemy soldiers, informers, and dogs raided the old crate on wheels in which R. was supposed to be, but they found only Xanthi there. When she was questioned by the Commandant, Xanthi said that she hadn't had any patrons or guests for a long time, and knew nothing about anyone named R.

15. R. began to worry that the Allied Headquarters might be infiltrated by enemy agents.

THE
REAL
STORY

"And about time too," chortled Tryfos.

"Has anyone figured out yet who R. might be?" asked Old Petros.

"Whoever he is, he's too naïve to be still alive," said Kyr Notis.

"Oh, he's alive, all right," said Old Petros.

"Does that mean there is more coming our way?" asked Tryfos.

"Have no doubt," said Old Petros. "But don't worry, I am through for now."

"Good!" said Tryfos. "Now that you are through the second part of the true story, how about the conclusion of the *real* story?"

"To be fair, I guess you've earned it," conceded Old Petros. "Now, where was I?"

"Where the Coast Guard officers went to bring the old bugger before the Governor," said Tryfos.

"Yes, that's where you stopped," confirmed Aris.

". . . and so when the Governor saw the old fucker standing in front of him and trembling, he said, 'I have seen everything that you tried to do on that rock, and all I want to know is Why? . . . And I want the truth!' Well, that scared the shit out of the poor bastard. 'You really saw everything?' he asked, his hands shaking. Instead of speaking, the Governor handed him the spyglass. 'It's no use,' confessed the old rascal, 'I'll tell everything.' He told the whole story of his life: his regular excursions to the rock island, his sinning—that's how he put it—with the boys from the boarding school, and his noticing how one after another they all became prosperous and famous, but he remained a wretch. 'So I thought of doing it to myself for a change,' he said, 'to see if I could also benefit from it, that's all.' The Governor was laughing. 'Well, did you do it?' he asked. 'Just a little,' confessed the other. 'It's not easy, you know.' 'Yes, of course,' said the Governor, and he laughed until tears came to his eyes. At the end he said, 'I trust you remember that I too tasted those figs on the rock with you when I was a student at the boarding school. . . . Here, have some of mine.' He offered him some of the fresh figs on the table, but the old man was too scared to eat any. 'Don't be afraid,' said the Governor, patting his bent back. 'Rejoice. Beginning today, I, on behalf of the State and in gratitude for your innumerable diverse services, order that you be the recipient of a modest pension, so that you may live the remaining years of your life in dignity and comfort.' The dirty old man couldn't believe his ears. But the expression on the face of the Governor was more than reassuring. Finally the old man said, 'It's awesome, isn't it?' The Governor didn't understand. 'It works! It works, is what I mean,' shouted the old man. 'Don't you see? I only managed to touch my prick to the right asshole, my asshole, and in less than an hour I get a pension for life. What, I wonder, would have happened if my prick were a bit younger and longer?' "

On the way back, I asked Aris how the old man who'd screwed all those nice-looking boys from the boarding school related to his theory of mosquito bites?

"He doesn't relate," said Aris. "He's a pervert."

XVII

Later that week, Aris learned from Chryssa that Lemonia and Angelica had just left to spend the rest of the summer in the Pine Forest with relatives. Aris and I agreed to take a little trip there to see how the girls were doing.

XANTHI

With Angelica gone, I saw no point in going to church the following Sunday. Instead, I walked over to the square to visit Xanthi, who lived in the old crate on wheels. Xanthi was surprised to see me at her door.

"What are you up to?" she said without opening the door all the way.

I looked around, afraid that someone might see me. "I've come to ask you a favor," I said.

"You've never been here to see me before, have you?"

"No, I haven't."

"How come?"

"There have been scary stories—the actors' disease, the old crate."

"Lies," she said, "but get your ass in. It's cooler indoors."

It was dark inside the crate. As my eyes adjusted, I noticed the old stage sets stacked against the right wall and the dusty, still colorful costumes of the actors on the left, hanging from a row of nails. Xanthi sat on her bed next to the costumes, and with her foot she pointed to a wooden stool behind the door.

"Sit your ass down," she said. And she said, "What's on your mind? Come on, speak up. I'm too weak for guessing games."

"I want to know all about love," I said.

"Love. Isn't that something! Tell me, who sent you here?"

"Nobody. I've come on my own."

"Then what made you think that I know all about love? Don't you even know the difference between straight love and straight screwing?"

"I'm not talking about love for your mother and father and all that," I said.

"You're talking about men and women."

"Yes."

"And you're also talking about screwing, no?"

"I guess so."

"Sorry, I can't help you," she said.

"Why?"

Xanthi was silent. A sliver of light that came from a crack between the boards of the crate crossed her left cheek like a scar.

"Why?" I asked again.

"Because I've forgotten everything that's good about it, and the bad things won't matter to you."

"Tell me anyway."

"Go home. I'm too weak for that shit."

"Won't you at least tell me something?"

"Like what?"

"Tell me what's a honeymoon. What is it that women do with men after the wedding until they get pregnant?"

"They do a lot of screwing, for one."

"I mean, besides screwing. Why do they call it honeymoon?"

"They call it honeymoon because it has a spread of honey all over it—that's what makes it glow. But it doesn't last long. You see, beneath that layer of honey the moon is full of shit. . . . Anyway, right after the wedding, the men and the women spend a month or so licking the honey, and then the women get pregnant, and all the honey is gone."

"And then? What happens then?"

"You asked me to tell you about the honeymoon. I did. That's all there is to be said. Everything else is shit."

Aris knocked on the door before dawn, and I was ready in a few minutes. "It's going to take more than seven hours to get to the Pine Forest by foot, so the earlier we start off, the better," said Aris. I put on an old pair of sandals, my shorts, a tee shirt, and a frayed straw hat that Grandmother used to wear when she picked okra in the good times, and I ran after Aris in the dark.

By sunrise we'd already left the fields behind and had taken a shortcut through mountainsides, ravines, and dried-up creeks. We were thirsty. The ravines were strewn with rifle shells, and twice we saw in the distance human remains covered with carrion birds. Then we passed through a field of ancient ruins, and Aris said, "We'll probably spend the night here on the way back." And he said, "This is where the Mountain Fighters gather before a battle, to swear 'Freedom or Death.' Chances are they're watching us right now," he said. "Where from?" I asked. "Over there," he said, pointing to the ragged mountain peak. "But don't worry. Capetan Andromache has already figured out who we are and where we're heading."

We peeled a few thistle stems for lunch, and pressed on. We were thirsty. Aris said that we were supposed to meet Lemonia and Angelica at a little spring. "So don't lose your thirst before we get there," he said. I imagined the little spring bubbling thoughtlessly in the cool shade of the pine trees. Since it was the only spring in the area, all the paths in the forest met there, and Angelica's relatives had made a monument out of it: a block of white marble that tamed the thoughtless water through the mouth of a leaping fish, or the penis of a presumptuous cupid. And on the base of the marble block, the eternal inscription: DRINK TRAVELER.

"Lemonia's teeth make me think about water," said Aris. "People are talking about lips, but I am telling you, it's her teeth that make me think about water." Aris' lips were dry, chapped, and at the ends of his lips the ends of his words were white and gummy. "God, I am thirsty!" he said.

The forest was nothing but a grove of scrawny little pines, and the spring was dry.

LOVERS   We heard voices and steps approaching. At the turn of the path we saw Lemonia and Angelica. They walked slowly, holding hands. We rose and dusted off our pants and shirts. Angelica looked pale and weak. Lemonia, on the contrary, was healthy, with tanned skin and red cheeks. And then the dying trees exhaled a whisper of resin, and the spring didn't matter.

Aris and Lemonia walked ahead of us. We could hear them talk about life in the town, as if Lemonia were missing it, and then about the strangeness of forests in the evening hours. After the sunset and before the stars appeared, Lemonia felt lonely and strong. "How can you feel lonely and strong? When I am lonely I feel diminished; I feel thirsty, and embarrassed for feeling thirsty." Lemonia was silent then, as if she were blushing, and Aris took her hand, saying, "Nothing wrong with that." But that was beyond Angelica, who wanted to know everything and had no patience for anything that she couldn't explain.

"I have to sit down now, if you don't mind," she said.

"Are you all right?"

"Yes, but the doctor said I should rest often."

A period of awkward silence, during which Angelica and I saw Aris and Lemonia leave the path and walk among the trees, still holding hands. We looked each other in the eyes, and I blushed, but Angelica smiled. The same smile as the one she'd given me outside the church.

"Is it true that you made my picture with pebbles?" she asked.

I nodded.

"Like a mermaid, with a fish's tail?"

I nodded.

"How did you know?"

"Mosquitoes."

"How did you find out that I am a mermaid?"

I pointed to the blue veins under the pale skin of her throat and cheeks. "Because instead of blood you have the sea in your veins."

I thought she would laugh, but she didn't. I could see the blue veins throb beneath her skin. "I bet your blood is salty," I said.

"How did you know?"

"The veins under your skin," I said.

"During the night, and whenever I am alone, I turn into a mermaid," she said. "But you're the first one to suspect it."

I was embarrassed.

"Are you thirsty?" she asked.

I was silent.

"Are you embarrassed for being thirsty?" she asked.

I was embarrassed.

"My legs and feet become a fishtail," she said. "I

can swim very fast and stay underwater for a long time."

I was silent.

"When I see ships sailing by, I ask the sailors whether or not Alexis the poet still lives. If they say, 'He lives, he rules the oceans,' I grant them safe passage," she said.

"And if they say that he's drowned?"

Angelica's eyes shone with anger. "Then I stir the sea and wreck their ship, so they'll drown also."

"How do you know about Alexis?"

"That's a secret," she said. She got up, and we started to walk again. Suddenly, we saw Aris and Lemonia embracing behind a tree. We walked back and sat by the dried-up spring, waiting.

"Do you want to be my lover?" Angelica asked after a long silence.

I nodded.

She took something from her pocket and put it in my hand. It was a small white shell. I searched my own pockets desperately. I could find nothing besides my pencil and notebook. I offered her the notebook. Angelica came closer and kissed me on the cheek.

A
HIDING
PLACE
On the way back, Aris said that he had no doubt that Lemonia's heart was in the right place, thank God, but for the time being she could not go against her father's will, so they'd have to wait. Aris wasn't impatient or unhappy. He said that with time everything was going to work out all right. He was talking to himself, not soliciting my reaction, and only after a two-hour monologue did he ask me what Angelica and I did all the while he was with Lemonia.

By nightfall we reached the ancient ruins where we planned on staying until the next morning.

"Now, according to the instructions," said Aris,

standing between two solitary rusty columns, "ten steps eastward from here"—he took ten steps eastward and stopped—"should be a white marble slab covered with dirt and dry weeds." He swept the ground with his foot, revealing the white marble. "Well!" he said triumphantly.

At the same time we heard the sound of stones nearby: "Tap-tap, tap-tap." It was like a signal for something, and Aris quickly covered the slab with dirt. We sat on a step between the two columns, silently, trying to listen for more sounds. When a few more minutes went by without incident, Aris said, "Under that slab, there are steps going deeper down, to a large room. It's safe and cool there, but very dark."

"Well?"

"If we stay up here, I'm afraid somebody's going to take a shot at us. So I thought maybe we should go down there. Others have used it as a hideout before. But it's dark."

"I'm not afraid."

We went back to the slab, and Aris cleared it off again. "There's something else you should know," he said as he stooped to push the marble slab aside. "This place was a tomb in the old times."

"Oh."

"But it doesn't have skeletons and such."

"What about buried treasure?"

"I've heard there was plenty of gold here in the past, but others have already grabbed it. Archeologists, they call them."

As we moved the slab aside, we heard the signal again: "Tap-tap, tap-tap."

"Hurry up," said Aris, making way for me to step down.

"You first," I said.

"I've got to go last so I can pull the slab over the hole again," he whispered impatiently.

I stepped down cautiously onto the top of a narrow stair and started climbing deeper into the dark. At the same time, I heard a noise coming from outside, and when I looked up, I saw two shadows gagging Aris and lifting him away, and the slab sliding back into place, covering the opening completely. I panicked, shouted, tried to push the marble, but I lost my balance and fell.

IN
A
KING'S
TOMB

Lower in the night, low, where there is neither light nor reflection thereof, and the shell of the tomb's dome is invisible, where the roots of the singing trees thicken, shivering, there was something I knew not, I touched it and knew it had died, it was still warm, death was still there. I touched it, buried it, so late in the night it was I could invent no names to name it. I moved past words, past my own wounds, hands moving past their own memories: this is the limit. I turned back—no light there either.

Alexis went on reciting, but there was no voice coming out of his mouth, and then his mouth too was filled with darkness. I felt a throbbing pain in my head, and opened my eyes. Still dark. How long had I been down there? I put my hand in my pocket to find out if the little white shell was in one piece. It was. I brought it close to my eyes, and after concentrating on it for a while, I was able to see its faint glow. Since the tomb was sealed, that glow proved that the little shell had its own source of light. I put it carefully back into my pocket, and slowly got up. Head throbbing, ribs aching, right knee bleeding, left hand numb. Light hand rising, fingers tracing words on a stone: "Oros Eimi"—"Milestone," or "Limit." Lower down, clay jars for wine and oil, all filled with dark. If they killed Aris, they'd never find me. Grandmother's eyes would dry up completely, and she'd never even see my shadow filling the house. The sea would swell and recede, rearranging the colored pebbles on the sand: a finger here, a strand of black hair, a green almond there, and the fragments of an old crushed tile—lips and nipples of a pale pink. Who'd reassemble all this? "He's dead, he's dead," would reply the sailors. "He reigns in a king's tomb." But Angelica would stir the sea and send their ship to the bottom. I swooned, closed my eyes, and dreamed that the slab of the tomb had been removed again, and I was rising toward the exit, where Phlox waited for me patiently.

"Are you all right?" said Aris.

"He's fine," said the man who carried me.

I opened my eyes once more and saw the faces of several Mountain Fighters who stood by, dark against the lucent sky above the eastern ridge.

My wounds healed quickly, but for many weeks I had dizzy spells and fever, and I could not sleep for more than a few minutes at a time. Grandmother said that when I fell down the stairs into the tomb and hit my head, my brains got all shaken up, so I'd better stay in for a while and take it easy. Each time I awoke during the night, I thought I was still trapped in the tomb, and once, for no reason that I could think of, I began to hit my head against the wall so hard that by the time Grandmother woke up and stopped me, blood was trickling down my face

GRANDMA
ON
MEMORY

and neck, and there was a red smudge on the wall. That night I cried out loud for a long time. In the morning Grandmother said that by hitting my head against the wall I'd probably shaken my brain back to the right place, which meant that I would soon be all right. She also said that I should try not to forget the details of my accident and what I was afraid of while I waited to be rescued. Nor should I forget the thoughts that were connected with it, or the dreams I'd had since then. "Because if you do forget them, a good part of you would be trapped in that tomb forever," she said. I started writing down everything on a sheet of paper, but I couldn't remember very much, and I soon realized that I was making up most of the dreams and stories, so I decided to stop writing and start using my shadow puppets instead.

XVIII

When Angelica came back from the Pine Forest, her health, instead of improving, deteriorated. The doctor said that he couldn't do anything to help her, and a week or so later, Aris, who had just seen Lemonia secretly, came over to return my notebook.

"Lemonia said you can go to the wake tonight, if you want to." He avoided my eyes, and, turning around, he started down the steps, adding, "The funeral will be tomorrow afternoon."

"Are you crazy?" I shouted to him, but he didn't respond. I sat down and tried to recall Angelica's face, her features one by one. I saw her smiling. The small white pebbles of her teeth, the blue sea in the veins of her neck and cheeks. Then I tried to imagine her dead, but her eyes and lips wouldn't close, the sound of her voice wouldn't stop. Then I saw the flowers all around her face and body, but her face and body were missing. The priest put a cross on her chest, but the cross lay on the bottom of the casket, which was a small boat. Three old women, who had sung praises and lullabies to her after her mother died, now wailed, their gray heads swaying between their shoulders. But the boat was empty except for the cross and the flowers, which began to smell stronger as they wilted in the warm air.

"Whose wake? Whose funeral?" I shouted at Aris as he turned around the corner, but he didn't respond. "You are crazy," I said, and I got up and went to the sea, and the sea swelled and receded, leaving only the wrinkled, dried-up crust of its surface on the bottom of the small bay.

THE COLOR OF THE MOUNTAIN

The end of that summer was marked by a strange event. A few days after Angelica's death, the sun and the sky turned yellow, and the light seemed to pass through a haze of sulphur. People, houses, roads, even the sea, looked yellow, and even our shadows—a darker yellow on yellow. Then the blind old singer was struck with horror as even his darkness turned yellow—a deep, deep yellow like gold. No one in town could explain what had happened. The doctor wondered whether or not that yellow light were here to stay, and if it were, how it would affect our lives. To me, people already seemed to move about in a slower rhythm and to talk less, as though something else were constantly on their minds. Then Barba-Rotas, who had an evil eye, predicted the end of the world, saying that the yellow light was the most terrible sign he'd ever seen. My cousin Aris had his own theory. He remembered that on the map our region was always shown in yellow color, and he said, "I bet every region in the country actually took the color with which it had been represented on the map for so many years." Accordingly, the Northern Region was pink, the Central beige, the Western lilac, the Southern green, and the Islands white. It was an interesting theory, but not a convincing one, and several neighbors laughed at Aris, saying that even Barba-Rotas' theory seemed more likely than his.

To prove he was right, Aris decided to take a trip south. His mother, my aunt, didn't approve of his decision, but his father, though sick in bed, thought Aris had an obligation to prove his theory, therefore he should go. "That's it," said Aris, putting a change of clothes in a bag; and Philippos and I decided to go with him as far as the fields, to see him off from there.

As we were leaving the house, my aunt said, "I don't know what the color of the south is, but I know the color of the mountain, and I warn you: that color is *red*. Don't go to the mountain."

Philippos and I escorted Aris to the fields, and, sitting on a hillside, we watched him take the trail to the mountain and slowly disappear into the yellow weeds and thistles.

On our way back, while crossing Grandmother's field, Philippos and I stopped to see if my father's hideout was still preserved. Less than three years back, when the wheat had just begun to sprout, I dug a three-by-six hole so my father could have a place to hide in when the enemy and the informers were after him. I dug it up well and covered it all over with branches, leaves, and dirt, on top of which I planted more wheat for camouflage. My father couldn't find the spot. "What's the use of it if I can't find it easily," he'd said. And he'd said, "On the other hand, you may be right. If I can find it just like that, it wouldn't be a very safe place to hide." I was glad that he'd considered that, but I was also embarrassed for having forgotten to leave an opening so he could go in and out. In the end, he had to lift one side of the roofing, but when he'd gotten in and lain down, sure enough, his body fit exactly.

Philippos and I couldn't find the spot. Either the roof had collapsed and the hole filled with soil, or it

A
HIDING
PLACE
FOR
FATHER

still held, covering the hole as it was meant to, preserving and protecting it even from myself, like a little bubble beneath the surface of the earth, which at one time had contained my father, and it was filled with his panting.

XIX

On Sunday afternoon, Grandmother called Philippos, Flisvos, and myself into the house, and gave each one of us a cracker. "I am giving you this to keep your mouths busy, so you can listen for a moment without interrupting," she said.

KITE-MAKERS AND CRACKER-EATERS

"Where did you get these, Grandma?"

She turned around and opened the door to the basement, saying, "Come upstairs. They're all here."

A tall bearded man of about thirty-five years walked up to us and said, "Yes, I am None. You can call me None." His beard, his body odor, and his clothing left little to the imagination. We walked around him to see if he carried a gun.

"Sit still and listen," ordered Grandmother.

'"Let me start with a question," said the man who wanted to be called None. "How many of you know how to make a kite?"

All three of us raised our hands. "Star-shaped kites," I said.

"Now, how many of you can keep a secret?" said None.

"All three of them," said Grandmother, "or I'll pluck their ears."

"Fine," said None. And he said, "Kite-makers and secret-keepers ought to be cracker-eaters."

We applauded.

"Sh . . . Fine," he said. "Now listen. I want you to make the largest kite you can—star-shaped or moon-shaped, but large. Say four strides in diameter."

"Any size," said Flisvos.

"Any size, but we'd need to have cord and paper," said Philippos.

"I will bring the cord and the paper; you'll get the straws for the frame," said None.

"What about glue?" I said. "We'd need glue to stick the paper to the frame and to the cord."

"You're right," said None, "but where can one find glue these days?"

"We can make good glue from crackers," said Flisvos.

The man whose name was None thought we were joking, so Philippos offered to explain: "We can make a paste with crackers by chewing them. It takes longer to dry, but when it does, it holds like glue."

None smiled. "Once you put the crackers into your mouth," he said, "can you get yourself to spit them out again?"

"If we have a whole box of crackers, we'll make sure to spit out enough glue for the kite," promised Flisvos.

THE
MISSION

Next morning, Grandmother handed us a sheaf of red sheets of paper, a ball of parachute cord, and a half box of crackers. "You'll get the other half box when you've finished the kite," she said. We set to work by pulling three bamboo straws from Grandmother's fence. We cleaned them, cut them to size, and joined them in the middle, forming a star-shaped frame. We spread the ends at equal distances from each other and tied a string around them, turning the star into a perfect hexagon. We attached the sheets, clipped them to size, covering the frame. Used every other cracker to make glue. The tail had to be some sixteen strides long. We folded more sheets of paper, shredded them with a pair of scissors, tied the shreds along the string of the tail. We used the same method to make the "beard," that's three pieces of string attached to the center of the frame and to the two upper beams. We stretched the beard, and at its peak we fastened the end of the ball of parachute cord. By noon the glue had dried, and the box of crackers was empty.

The kite was enormous and had an overwhelming pull. Even when it flew low, it took more than one of us to hold it still. None showed up with the rest of the crackers, and advised us against releasing the entire length of the cord. We pulled the kite down and went in.

"Here's the rest of it," said None. "I want you to take the kite down to the shore and wait until sunset. If the wind changes from southwest and blows from the north, as it usually does in the afternoon, you will fly the kite and get in one of those small fishing boats. Now, if the wind's strong enough, you won't even have to work on the oars; the wind will push the kite, and the kite will pull your boat straight to the minefield."

Did he say "minefield"? We looked at each other, and then at Grandmother, disbelieving.

"Don't worry," said None. "The mines are quite a bit below the surface. There's no danger of running into one. Now listen. If the wind is too strong, you might have to use the oars to slow down, otherwise you might drift all the way to the concrete ships. If for any reason you can't control it, it's best to let the kite go. If things go well, when you reach the minefield look at the red cans floating in a row, and you'll see one of them is painted green. Tie the end of the kite line to the chain underneath that can, and return to the shore as fast as possible. Then straight back home, and not a word to anyone. Do you think you can do it?"

It sounded fairly easy, but it didn't make sense. Once again we looked at Grandmother.

"All right," said None, "I will tell you why we want to do this. Of course, by the time you get back to shore it will be dark, and the enemy won't see much of the kite, but tomorrow morning everybody will see it from the concrete ships, and the enemy will get the message that our spirit runs high."

"What if the patrol boat comes before we get to the green can?"

"You will say that you wanted to go to the concrete ships and trade your kite for bread."

"And what if they don't believe us?"

"Then give them the kite as a present, and return home."

"If they suspect us they will take us prisoner," said Flisvos.

"Disregard what they say, and keep begging for bread."

We went through the details once more, and tried to memorize the most important ones: north wind, sunset, speed of sailing, green can, bread-bread-bread, and not a word to anyone about None, the kite, or the crackers.

THE
END
OF
THE
WORLD

The wind changed, and during the rest of the afternoon it gathered strength and remained favorable. When we flew the kite, the pull turned out to be stronger than we needed it to be, so we held the oars down and still, slowing the boat. The wind took us almost straight to the green can, onto which we fastened the end of the cord, just in time. If we'd arrived there five minutes later, it would have been too dark to tell between red and green. As we pulled on the oars and made for the shore, we saw the kite pulling the can toward the ships, and we thought that was strange, since each mine was chained to a stake in the bottom of the sea.

The shore was deserted, except for the old blind musician, who sat on the pebbles talking to his dog. As we passed in a hurry, he turned his face and followed us with his white eyes.

Just before reaching the first houses, we saw a flash that flooded the sky and the town with white light. Then we felt a sudden gust of wind from the sea, and heard an explosion, followed by a prolonged reverberation like rolling thunder. Heavy debris began to rain around us, and we took cover under a small bridge. At that moment, another flash, another violent gust, another explosion. And then another, and another, and now and then two or three at a time. Each gust of wind brought clouds of black smoke. Huge chunks of steel and concrete were falling all over. The sky glowed with twisting flames. And in the light of the flames we saw columns of smoke billowing from the direction of the concrete ships.

"Maybe the war will be over after this," said Philippos, trembling.

"Maybe the world has come to an end," whispered Flisvos, rubbing his good eye.

What happened? / No one knows; I think it's the submarines. / Impossible. / Why not? / The entrance of the bay is blocked with wire networks, and the ships protected with sea mines. / What's going on? / An accident, maybe. / The sea is still burning. . . . You can read a newspaper in the middle of the night. / Got a newspaper? / All my windows are smashed. / Mine too. / My dog was howling all afternoon—no wonder. / Maria, the children! / Have you heard anything on the radio? / Sh . . . / If the Allies don't land by morning, there will be mass executions. . . . Maybe we should take to the

CONFUSION
AND
FEAR

133

mountain. / The swine will burn down the whole city. / Better get in and lock the door. / Put out the light. / Have you seen a little gray kitten? / What? Are you— / Maria, the children!

Within an hour's time a convoy of enemy tanks and trucks full of soldiers arrived from the nearest camp, surrounding the town. No one allowed to enter or depart. A twenty-four-hour curfew, and a house-to-house search. Shooting at random.

No, we haven't seen anyone looking suspicious. / Say, "Suspicious, sir." / Suspicious, sir. / All right, round them up! / Please, don't take me away; I am a law-abiding citizen. / And I have small children, and a sick old mother. / Take them! / Maria, where are the children? / Take him away too. / Where? Where? . . . / It's got to be the Allies. / Why the Allies? / I'm telling you, tomorrow morning there will be an invasion—ships, planes, tanks. / Why the Allies? Aren't our Mountain Fighters capable of teaching the swine a lesson? / Sh . . . / Long live the Mountain Fighters! / Shut up.

HELL'S FIRE   The explosions had killed all the fish in the bay; and as the fire went on for three days on the surface of the sea, enemy soldiers from the concrete ships were washed ashore burnt, blackened, torn. The enemy picked up the bodies and buried them. We picked up the fish, but they were soaked in kerosene, and we had to throw them out again. We also found sacks of flour, but that too was too oily and salty to eat. There were arrests, interrogations. Then the Commandant warned us that fifty men would be executed if the town didn't come up with the actual saboteurs. But the informers spread rumors that the Commandant planned to burn the town to the ground, and to kill or deport the population.

A week went by. When the deadline expired, the

enemy took thirty of our men to the quarry. The news about the burning of the town persisted for another week. Finally, the Commandant declared that it had to be either the town or the remaining twenty men, and asked us to choose. We refused to, and the next morning the twenty were taken to the quarry.

Walking along the edge of the sea, I saw the remnants of our kite: half-burnt, discolored shreds of paper, split straw, the broken cord. The sky was gray, and the sea black. The concrete ships were no longer there. I was cold. On my way home, I heard the sound of a guitar playing, and I stopped. The music came from a ruined house. I went close, looked behind a half-torn wall, and saw the blind old man. Slowly, he turned his face in my direction, and stared at me with blank eyes. His little dog whined at me. The old man stroked the dog's head, and began to play his guitar and to speak: "The sky was yellow and only a single kite, blood-red, star-shaped, shone in the air. The sea was yellow and only a single buoy, green like a sea plant, shone among the waves. And where the star went, the plant followed steadily. Under the plant, under the surface of the water, hell's fire, smoke, and storm followed, trapped in iron."

Next morning, the old man was found dead in that ruined house. Still sitting, eyes wide open, a void, mouth still open, the song still echoing in the dark of his mouth, hands resting on his knees, the guitar on the ground. The dog sat on the guitar, whining. Philippos, Flisvos, several other kids, and I leaned against the wind with our hands in our pockets, watching. We were still alive, barely alive. The surviving bones wrapped in brittle skin, the bellies swollen and empty. Dirty. Diseased. Injured. And the clothes coming apart, the tatters held together

THE
OLD
SINGER
DIES

with wire stitches. When the skin itself opened up, it did not heal. Silent against the wind that whistled, our hands in our pockets, we watched the trash wagon carry the old singer out of town. He lay on top of the refuse, and the dog was following— the dog, a perpetual mourner.

ONE
MORE
SPRING

The mountaintops were covered with snow, and the Mountain Fighters came down to the lower caves, harassing the enemy for food and weapons. The little fires that kept increasing on the mountainside, the little fires that glowed at night around the mountain, were lit by the Mountain Fighters. "One more spring, one more summer at the most," I heard someone say. I turned, but couldn't tell where the voice had come from. Flisvos and Philippos hadn't heard a word.

"One more spring, one more summer at the most," I said.

"But that would make it a year, wouldn't it?" said Flisvos.

We saw a little fire flicker on the mountainside, and we stretched our hands toward it to warm them.

XX

The northwest wind brought dried-up thistles and
tumbleweeds from the desolate fields. And it
brought the wandering bird that once was a gypsy
called Socrates. Socrates traveled on foot, selling a
hundred kinds of spices and herbs. "He must cover
a large part of the country," said Aunt Zoë, because
he came to our town only once a year, around
okra-picking time. His clothes and sandals were always dusty, his brow sweating, and his voice—Ah,
that voice, echoing through the neighborhoods:
cinnamon, marjoram, saffron—a hundred kinds of
spices—bay leaves, oregano, thyme, and camomile. He'd stop for a glass of water, then take the
opportunity to describe his goods more intimately
and to offer samples, which the women rubbed
gladly between their palms, then sniffed or tasted.
Childless wives would shyly ask his opinion about
this or that herb and its invigorating properties, or
its use concerning fertility, but Socrates didn't seem
to encourage speculation. But then he sympathized
with their problem, and didn't discourage them altogether. Once I overheard him relate a story according to which scrapings from an ancient sculpture of an oversized phallus in a field outside a

neighboring village could bring about pregnancy. "You're supposed to mix these scrapings with warm wine," he said, but he wouldn't guarantee the prescription. "One day I actually saw that marvelous sculpture," he said. "It was rising from a field of poppies like a white cannon. All around its barrel I could see dozens of scratches and inscriptions of vows, initials, and thanks. Then I was told that even my own mother had thought of trying some scrapings in her wine. She was married for three years, but still hadn't had any children, and she thought she wouldn't lose anything by giving it a try—not that she really believed in it. But then I was told that when she got married to my father she was only twelve," said Socrates.

Cinnamon, clover, marjoram, basil, saffron, rosemary, bay leaves, mountain tea, oregano, fennel, red and black pepper, hemlock, thyme, allspice, mint, camomile. How much this time? Uncle Spanos and Aunt Zoë would buy a lot of it, and Socrates knew why. The priest had recommended camomile to all unmarried people, and Socrates said, "Of all the things that priest preaches, only what he says about the camomile is true." Camomile was supposed to soothe all kinds of inflammations and irritations, even Satan's tickle, which afflicted the private parts of the body. When Aunt Zoë bought her year's supply, Socrates said to her, "Actually, many people love camomile tea for its fine taste, and others drink it to soothe an upset stomach, or to get rid of a hangover. But this time of year, everyone is using it to get relief from the okra rash," he said.

OKRA Okra and okra plants sting, that's no secret. They don't sting as badly as the nettles, but you'd do well not to walk in a field of okra without long pants and shoes. We planted okra at the same time as the tomato, and harvested the pods every other day from July through September. Men and women wrapped their fingers in rags during picking, to avoid the itching rash that the little hairs of the okra can cause. Stewed with fresh tomato, onion, olive oil, and herbs, the pods made a delicious meal, and there were people swearing that it's even an aphrodisiac. But Old Petros said, "Thereby hangs a tale, and that goes as far back as the First Great Famine, during which men, lacking the necessary energy for sex, rubbed their genitals with okra leaves, which caused inflammation and long-sustained erections. That's why several dozen kids who were born around that time, and are now my son's age, came down in history as the Okra Breed."

The northwest wind whistled through the bamboo fence of our yard. Grandmother had gone to sleep early, saying, "If you look for it on the table and can't find it, look for it in bed." I leaned against the wall, half asleep, listening to Grandmother talk in her dream. She said, "Oh, why not let a few useless weeds grow in the mirror?" I was struggling not to go to sleep so I could hear what she might come up with next. Then I heard a "meow." Was there a kitten in Grandmother's dream? "Meow." Out there the wind was cold, full of shuddering whispers running through the useless weeds and the straw. Dark yellow eyes, ruffled fur, body twisting to resist the wind, head-on to the wind. The moon, a small copper coin, came out of the clouds, and the kitten was on top of the bamboo fence, fighting the wind on the wind's terms. "Meow." An acrobat who's brave enough to walk on wire, but afraid of climbing down. As I approached, he hissed at me and raised a paw to attack me. I turned around, offered my shoulder. He jumped, he tried to find his balance, his claws in my skin. I slapped him, and he

MEOW

139

bit at my earlobe. He was skinny. His underbelly hung loose, and there was nothing between skin and bones. I took him in. He meowed, purred, licked my earlobe, then bit it again. "Sorry, there's nothing to eat." He began to lick his own fur, then to chew on the blanket.

Grandmother was still dreaming. "Who's there?" she asked, without opening her eyes.

"It's me, Grandmother."

"Useless," she said.

XXI

Uncle Spanos died in April, and his sister, Zoë, followed him a few days later. The neighborhood girls dressed Aunt Zoë in a wedding gown embroidered years ago, when she was young herself and hoped to marry sometime, and she was buried as a bride. I went to the funeral carrying a bunch of camomile flowers mixed with red anemones. The old teacher didn't show up for the eulogy, as she was still bedridden. I stayed in the cemetery after everyone else had left, and I walked around reading names and dates on the wooden crosses. Most of the graves were recent, most of the deaths caused by hunger, some by disease, some by both. The hanged and the gunned-down were buried where they had met their death—in many cases, after having dug their own graves at gunpoint.

As I turned around, I saw someone peeking from behind a mound and a cross, and I shuddered. As I approached carefully, a man came out into the open, aiming at me with his rifle.

"Halt! Who goes there!"

"Aris!"

We embraced. His body or that strange uniform he had on gave off a heavy odor, the odor of the

141

Mountain Fighters. He had a bullet wound in his left arm.

"I thought he was a baker, but he was a bugger," said Aris.

"Did you get him?"

He didn't answer. His father had been getting worse, and Capetan Andromache gave Aris permission to come down the mountain and visit his family secretly. We climbed up a cypress tree to hide until the sun went down, and the tree began to sing.

"I suppose it's for Aunt Zoë," I said.

"No, it's for my father," said Aris.

We closed our eyes, listening until dark, then took the path to our neighborhood. Aris hadn't washed for weeks. There was no water, and the wound in his arm made everything difficult. The Mountain Fighters rubbed their bodies with snow, but many got pneumonia. And as the enemy was always after them, there wasn't even time for their clothes to dry. Aris paused, looked at me and his younger brother, and said in a low tone of voice, "Some say this has nothing to do with washing or not washing; the stench that's with us is the stench of death." His mother, my aunt, shook her head and started to cry, saying, "Didn't I warn you? Didn't I tell you that you are not made to be a hero?" But my uncle was glad to see Aris become a man, and he died with a proud smile that same night. And when Aris came down the mountain again a few months later, his left arm was missing.

GROWING   Although the famine persisted, my body continued to grow, sometimes in spasms. I'd wake up in the morning and feel my skin stretched, cracking at the joints and in the corners of my mouth, bleeding, then taking a long time to heal.

"It's the bones that grow first," said Grandmother, "the bones stretching the skin. So if your

clothes don't fit anymore, we'll just have to tear
them a little, here and there," she said, "right where
the skin cracks—the skin being your first layer of
clothing."

Then the furniture began to shrink, and the
house, and objects that used to take both my hands
to carry now seemed small enough for one hand;
and when I found how hard it was to do a different
thing with each hand at the same time, I thought I
had a coordination problem, and I went back to
Grandmother for advice.

"I guess it's the brain that grows first," said
Grandmother, "the brain that pushes the bone that
stretches the skin. But the brain also lengthens your
tongue," said Grandmother. "So when the corners
of your mouth split, you can lick the corners of your
mouth—if you know what I mean," she said.

And I said, "I do."

"But that isn't all," said Grandmother. "You must
also remember to dip your tongue in your brain
every time your tongue is about to speak. Dip your
tongue in your brain before you speak, is what I
mean."

And I said, "I will." But it wasn't easy, and that
was another problem of coordination, as speech
kept on coming faster than thought.

I went to the old teacher for advice. She was glad
to see me. "Sorry there is nothing in the house to
treat you to. Your grandmother is a holy woman,"
she said; "strange and unpredictable, but holy yes,
and of course right about your brain. Well, I
wouldn't worry about it; your brain will catch up
with your tongue one day. Words are exhaustible,
but the brain is not. It will go on, and your tongue
will then follow slowly, stuttering, struggling, sweating . . . Such a pity there is nothing in the house to
treat you to but words." She paused, and I could tell

WORDS

143

she was trying to think up something else that would interest me. "Yes, a few years ago I was passing by your grandmother's house, I mean the old one, the house that she burned down, and I saw you playing in the front yard. . . . Yes, five or six years ago, and I greeted you: 'Good morning there.' You turned around, looked at me, and said, 'Good morning, ruffiana.' "

"I didn't know how to dip the tongue in the brain; I didn't know what that word meant. I liked the way it sounded but didn't know better. After you told Grandmother and you went your way, she called me in and ordered me to open my mouth: 'Say, *Aaaa*, let me see your tongue.' I said, *Aaaa*, and she threw a handful of pepper in my mouth. I choked; my tongue, gums, and throat swelled; they were covered with blisters that burned; I couldn't breathe. If you'd just heard that word for the first time, the way it sounded to me for the first time, you wouldn't have minded it, would you? But then Grandmother told me about it, and she said that among other things a ruffian is someone who goes and tells. So from then on, when I saw you, I called you ruffiana-ruffiana-ruffiana, but you couldn't hear it; only my tongue, my gums, and my throat could hear, because my mouth was always closed."

ALL
STORIES
ARE
GOOD

"What is it that makes older people want to relate anecdotes about the young? If it weren't for the pepper, I wouldn't remember the first time I said the word 'ruffiana,' but you'd remind me of it just the same, wouldn't you? And I'd listen with interest, even with pride: 'Did I? Did I really say that?' "

"And I would repeat that anecdote to you from time to time, and you would fill that early gap in your memory with my memory, grateful that I preserved it for you, thankful to find another stepping-stone each time you ventured another step into the dark of your early years." She paused, and I thought she looked weak. She made a great effort to talk, to keep her eyes open.

But I remembered. On my way to the store to buy lentils and vinegar, I was getting all worked up because the grocer was a foolish man. Besides feeling my ass every time I went to buy something, he also nibbled constantly and indiscriminately from his goods, as if he were trying to beat the flies to it. While chasing the flies with one hand, he'd stretch the other to pick an olive or an anchovy from the barrel, or a handful of roasted pumpkin seeds, which he ate without cracking and peeling, or— And his teeth were always filled with food, and his breath was so foul that I'd rather have him feel my ass than have him talk to me face to face. So when I walked in that day, I was glad to see that I was not alone with the grocer. The old teacher used to speak in a very special way when she was with other grown-ups, but only the doctor and a former lawyer really knew what her words meant. Others, including the grocer, were desperately trying to imitate her in order to prove that they too were educated, and they made fools of themselves. Well, the grocer must have had a rich, spicy lunch that day, because I saw him sweat and breathe heavily, and try to unbutton the collar of his shirt. And then, with hands full of pumpkin seeds and flies, he tried to unbutton his collar, saying, "I beg your most gracious pardon—oh dear—madam teacher, but—if I—ah—ghah—" I thought he was about to sneeze, but instead he collapsed on top of a sack of chickpeas, then on the floor, his face yellow like wax, chickpeas pouring all over his face. I looked at the teacher then, and she, who also knew our common unpretentious tongue, shook her head in regret and whispered, "He's had it."

The old teacher had fallen asleep with a faint smile on her lips, like a child put to bed with a story. Stories are good, I thought; all stories are good. Even if a story is about death, it's a good story. But death itself is not, there is no death that's a noble death. Asleep with a smile on her lips, as if she agreed: Death is obscene, all death is obscene. You touch the flies and you die. You touch the food and you die. You feel my ass, but in the next moment you die. While talking, while trying to speak, or while your teeth chatter with a violent yearning for food. Or silently with a faint smile on your lips, after having heard your favorite story, the one that says that all death is obscene. Time and again, the same old story, because every time it's different, more and more interesting. Chattering yes, or serenely with a smile so faint on your wrinkled lips: "ruffiana," or was it "putana"—such fantastic words! Well told, go now on tiptoe and close the door softly behind you; well told, besides, there's no pepper left in the house. Sorry there's nothing in the house to treat you to but words.

XXII

Uncle Iasson said that Lekas was jealous of the red-haired woman. "He doesn't let her out of the house, and he locks the door so no one can go in either. All day long she washes and perfumes her body, or combs her long hair in front of the mirror, waiting for Lekas. She probably despises him too," said Uncle Iasson.

When he talked about her, his voice was soft and deep, and he always stared at the ground. Grandfather worried that Uncle Iasson might get into trouble with Lekas over the red-haired woman. But when Grandfather went to lie down, Uncle Iasson moved closer, and I sensed that he wanted to talk more.

"Why does she wash and perfume her body all the time, Uncle?"

"I guess that's part of her agreement with Lekas. In return, he brings food and clothes for her. He gets those things from the enemy."

"What do they do when Lekas returns home in the evening?"

"They have dinner together, and then they go to bed, I guess."

"What do they do in bed?"

He glanced at me, smiling: "Sleep."

"What are you going to do about it, Uncle Iasson?"

"What would you do?"

"I'd kidnap her and take her to the mountain."

"Well!" he said, laughing. "Are you going to help?"

"What's in it for me?"

"Nothing, of course. It'll be a labor of love."

"The wall's high, studded with broken glass, and Lekas is waiting behind the window with a loaded rifle."

"Listen, I've written a letter," he whispered.

"Did you mail it to her?"

"Don't be silly. I want you to take it to her."

"But how?"

"First make sure that Lekas is not there. When you know that he's gone, knock on the door; and when she answers, slip the letter under the door. Simple," he said. "Then wait to hear what she has to say."

"What's in it for me?"

"Nothing. It's a labor of love."

ERMINA   I heard her voice, heard her voice, and remembered her lips. The sun was slipping behind a small white cloud, but her hair glowed, her hair, and the smooth skin of her knees. The dry leaves in her hair rustled then, and as some of them changed place, she picked one that she could feel touching her neck and offered it first to my uncle, then to me, confusing us. "No one is poorer than I," she said, "no one."

"Wait," she whispered, and as she read the letter behind the door, I heard her cry. "Thank you," she said at the end, and she said, "Come back tomorrow, will you? Same time." And then she asked my name. "Bread-lover and chocolate-worshiper," I

148

said, crossing my fingers. "Mine is Ermione, but you can call me Ermina," she said. And the next day she passed a thin chocolate bar together with a letter for my uncle under the door.

"Guess what's in it for me, Uncle Iasson," I said, licking my fingers, still brown and sticky from the chocolate.

"The letter," said Uncle Iasson with a trembling voice, his eyes shining wildly.

It was a long letter, which Uncle Iasson wouldn't read aloud, in spite of my threats to cease postal services. He read it slowly and to himself, having no ears for what I had to say; and when he finished reading and looked at me, he was looking past me, and gradually even his own skin and bones became transparent.

I sat on the steps thinking about him and Ermina: both faces hidden behind her hair, telling secrets, then kissing. She let her robe slip down. Lekas was a dark little grain of something, a crumb of paper, a hair under the covers. Ermina lifted the covers and dusted the bed, and my uncle took off his clothes and lay beside her. Both faces hidden in her long red hair, whispering kisses. Arms over arms, legs entwined, backs bending, flattening, stomachs rubbing, then the motion slowly changing, the breathing becoming panting. Their limbs sweating, their bodies rolling from back to back, then motionless as if they wished to listen to the soft sound of the sheets unwrinkling. Now his lips on her breast, hers at his ear, "Thank you, thank you," she says. And he says, "You'll go back tomorrow with another letter, won't you?"

"Where were you, Uncle?"

"Won't you?"

"Sure, Uncle Iasson."

XXIII

Philippos, Flisvos, and I named the kitten I'd found November. He liked heights. He loved to be on top of tables, bedposts, or cabinets, even on top of the door, which he then persuaded me to swing back and forth, and in response he quit meowing from hunger, and began to purr.

Philippos, Flisvos, and I decided to make a new kite from the leftover materials that None had provided earlier. Since very few kids had paper and cord to make kites for the spring competition, we thought that if the three of us combined know-how and talent, we had a good chance to win. In the old times, the trophy was a spring lamb, the gift of the mayor. The year before, there was no competition, and the Commandant was disappointed; so when the weather improved in April, he gave orders for a new competition to take place, and announced that the trophy would be a chicken.

When we test-flew our kite, November, the kitten, became excited, and he tried to climb my leg in order to reach the cord, and from there the kite.

"Let's fly him," said Flisvos.

"Fly him? The cat?"

"Why not? Just hang a little basket from the frame, and put him in." Flisvos went home and

150

came back with the basket. "Here," he said, "put him in."

As though he understood from the beginning, November jumped into the basket all by himself and began to purr.

"Let's go," said Philippos. He tied the handle of the basket to the center of the frame, and Flisvos helped him lift the kite high.

I took the spool and walked away from them some fifty strides. There was a brisk afternoon wind. The kite was large enough to carry the kitten. "Let go!" I shouted, pulling the line, and the kite rose, perfectly balanced between its beard and tail, which rustled against the clear sky. I let out more string, and the kite soared high above Flisvos and Philippos amid cheers and applause. As for the kitten, he wasn't the least scared. On the contrary, he seemed to be having the time of his life up there, looking down on us, bright orange eyes, paws resting on the lip of the basket, his cockpit.

"Let all the string go!" shouted Flisvos.

Word went around fast about November's flight, and several people began to ask when we might repeat the performance so they could watch too; but Flisvos, Philippos, and I kept answering. "A hungry cat won't fly."

We said, A hungry cat won't fly, but no one came up with bread, so we decided not to fly November before the kite festival. That way we could at least hope to win the competition and the Commandant's chicken. Then we heard that two other kids were also planning to introduce new features into the game: razor blades. Also, their father was an enemy collaborator, which meant they'd have access to first-class materials, such as thin but strong paper, real glue, brand-new razor blades, and parachute cord. They would arm their kite with razor blades with which they'd assault their competitors

COMBAT
TRAINING

151

and down the other kites by cutting their strings off. Slowly it became clear that the competition would turn into an air battle, therefore the winner would not be the most inventive and impressive kite, but the kite that would still fly after all the others had been downed. All the kids who'd signed up to participate went around looking for razor blades. We were concerned about November. Would he be able to defend himself and the kite from the razor blades? We could still pull out of the competition and save face. We decided to go on. We let November's claws grow, and we began to look for used razor blades. The ones we found were rusty and dull, but Grandmother improved them by sharpening their edges inside a glass. Afterward Philippos and I made a second kite, a dummy, and used it to train the kitten as a fighter. I held the big kite and the basket with the kitten in it, while Philippos attacked us with the dummy. It took November only a few minutes to figure out what was going on. First he was surprised and he ducked, hiding inside the basket. Then he stood up on his hind legs, ready to defend himself. I encouraged him to counterattack, and each time he ripped a piece of paper off the dummy I praised him, patting his head. Later we attached the razor blades to the dummy and repeated the training in order to make the kitten aware of the additional dangers of the game. He was learning fast.

FIRST
SKIRMISHES
On the day of the competition we waxed the cord and fastened the razor blades at the six ends of the frame and along the tail. We tied the handle of the basket to the center of the kite with thin wire for

extra security, and we walked to the top of the hill.

All in all, there were only a dozen kites competing. Most of them were star-shaped, but each one had a different color and size. Ours was red and one of the biggest. As soon as we reached the top of the hill, November jumped into his basket, and, seeing the other kites around him, he started to growl and to claw the air. It was a mild spring morning with a few small white clouds on the western horizon. The breeze that blew from the sea was strong enough to carry our kite and kitten high. When all the kites went up, with their armaments of razor blades glittering in the sun, the crowd cheered, then split into groups around their favorite competitors. By the time the first hostilities were under way, the enemy officers and soldiers had begun to place bets. Soon, all twelve kites were flying at about the same height, assaulting one another, maneuvering their way out of a tangle, or pulling up and releasing cord abruptly in order to make use of the blades along their tails.

I was approached and challenged from the left. It was a smaller but very agile kite that belonged to a kid a few years older than me. The crowd made room for him, then closed the circle around us. I gathered some of my cord, but the other managed to keep his kite just above mine, bringing his tail close to the knot that joined the main line with the beard. The crowd quieted down, and November rose on his hind legs, clawing the enemy tail and ripping some of its paper shreds, causing a wave of applause and praise. November had attracted the biggest crowd. The enemy kite climbed down to the same elevation, and Philippos shouted, "Watch out!" I passed the cord to my right hand, increasing the distance between the two kites. The enemy did the same, then took a step closer. The ends of our frames clashed so violently that November was almost thrown out of his cockpit. There was no damage to either kite, but the kitten, scared by the impact, remained hidden at the bottom of the basket. There were laughs. Once again I increased the distance between us by taking a step aside. At that moment the crowd was distracted by two other kites, which had gotten tangled and were heading downward with great circular leaps. When I noticed that my competitor was also absorbed by the spectacular fall, I pulled some of my cord and then released it again all at once, rubbing the entire length of my tail against his line. Seeing the danger from my move, the other released his own string, sending his kite away with such a jolt that his line snapped, and the kite itself flew off, then crashed in the fields. There was a prolonged cheer. Flisvos and Philippos began to dance, clapping their hands and shouting with joy, while my opponent gathered the rest of his string, sniffled, and went to pick up the remains of his kite.

THE
BATTLE
HEATS
UP

During the next half hour several more kites were downed, and the second round opened with five competitors: two against each other, and two against me. They approached me from right and left at the same time. They were twin brothers fighting as a team. Their father was an informer. The crowd became increasingly excited, especially the enemy officers and soldiers, who were betting heavily against me. Flisvos and Philippos were getting so worked up themselves that I found it hard to concentrate. When I didn't listen to their advice, they shouted at me with anger, and at least twice they tried to take the line away from me.

November rose again in his basket, but, seeing the enemy kites closing in from both sides, he ducked once more. Following the impact of the first strike from the right, he surfaced again, and, stretching his paw in the opposite direction, he started to claw the air. The audience laughed and

154

booed. Then one of the other two kites dueling nearby receded into the northern sky with severed strings. Followed by the entire group that surrounded him, the victor walked over and challenged one of the twins who harassed me from the left. There was a new wave of noise and betting. "Get him now," yelled Flisvos. I moved to the right quickly, and, pulling my cord down, I ran my frame blades 'along the back of the enemy kite. Nothing happened. But when I let the line go again before the other had a chance to maneuver around me, November stood up and clawed the enemy, ripping a long strip off his mainsail. "Bravo!" shouted the crowd.

The kid engaged with the other twin on my left suddenly crossed over to the right, sending his tail blades across the tail of his enemy. Fantastic move! The crowd quieted down, hands remained still in unfinished gestures, eyes fixed at the treacherous X of the two rows of razor blades sparkling against the bright blue of the sky. And then the twin's tail was slashed off, and we saw it recoiling, writhing like a wounded serpent. The crowd applauded, but the drama was not over yet. The tailless kite, having lost its balance, jerked upward over the victor's own kite, then headed straight down, dragging it along until both were smashed on the ground.

The pandemonium lasted for several minutes, during which the second group of spectators joined ours. Flisvos and Philippos fought to keep the crowd from closing in too much. I thought my op-

FINAL
DUEL

ponent and I had silently agreed to wait until the officers and the soldiers stopped betting and the crowd had quieted down, ready for the final duel. I was wrong. He moved swiftly, bringing his kite lower; and, raising his hand high, he sent his frame blades against my line. I pulled hard, closing in, and November reached out and tore another strip from the enemy's sail. The crowd quit betting, and several men pushed back to make room for maneuvering. I took two steps to the left and pulled my line further down. The other did the same. I raised my hand and took two steps to the right. He followed me again, and the ends of our frames clashed. The kitten fell down in his basket, but he reappeared instantly, and, seeing the enemy kite approach once more, he seemed ready to jump at it. My opponent pulled more string, then made an unexpected move: he came and sat in front of me, guiding his kite underneath and in front of mine. Before I could tell what he was up to, he raised his line high, bringing his frame blades against my cord. The crowd stopped breathing, and I could feel the friction of a razor blade. Any move was bound to increase that friction. And then something else happened: November took a leap against the enemy kite, and, clutching at its frame, he began to tear its sail ferociously with claws and teeth. Lighter without the kitten, my kite rose in the air away from the shining blades. The crowd responded with a deafening Aaaaah! Already, the enemy craft, with its sail torn to pieces, sinking under the weight of November, had lost half its altitude. My opponent pulled his line violently several times in a desperate effort to shake off the unexpected guest, but the kitten held fast, and within seconds kite and kitten were crash-landing in the fields.

It was a mild spring morning. The bright sunshine continued throughout the day as one by one even the small white clouds disappeared from the sky, and the cool breeze kept our kite flying above the neighborhood until sundown, when Grandmother called Philippos, Flisvos, myself, and November in to a dinner of roasted enemy chicken.

XXIV

RUMORS Aunt Anna owned an unregistered radio on which she could receive Allied broadcasts. Having an unregistered radio was illegal, and listening to such programs was punishable by death, but the informers hadn't been able to locate the radio, and Aunt Anna continued to be the best source of information. She only talked to those whom she could trust, and she never gave detailed accounts. "Good news, the Mountain struck again last night," she'd whisper to Grandmother. Or, "Bad news, the Allies say we shouldn't expect any help from abroad."

Grandmother was in bed with malaria, and Aunt Anna had come to take care of her and to wash our clothes.

"Hold on, Cousin," she said to Grandmother, placing a wet towel across her brow. "The Mountain Fighters are getting ready to deliver us, and the Allies are sending planes and ships to help the course of the war."

Grandmother was looking at me. "Tell him," she said weakly, "tell him to stay in. . . . I can't manage him anymore. Make sure that he stays in after you leave. . . . I can't even pull his ear anymore."

Aunt Anna came over and wrung my ear until I screamed. "There," she said.

158

"Why?" I asked. "Why?"

"Because your grandma is too weak to do it herself. And because I can tell that as soon as I leave you will walk out."

After Aunt Anna left, I went out to join Flisvos and Philippos, who were playing in the back yard of an abandoned house. I told them the news I'd heard from Aunt Anna, embroidered a little here and there: "Capetan Andromache is ready to come down the mountain and take the town. The Allies are sending shiploads of food."

"Are you sure?" said Philippos.

"I swear."

"I've heard that before," said Flisvos.

"I bet it's true," said Philippos. "Aris will be coming back."

"What are we going to do?"

"Let's do something. Anything," said Philippos.

"Like what?" said Flisvos.

"I don't know. How about ripping up the enemy flag on the roof of the old school?"

"Are you crazy?"

The next morning the enemy placed a big gun in the square and began to shell the mountainside.

"How about it?" said Philippos.

"How about what?"

"Ripping up the enemy flag and raising ours."

"No."

"Maybe we should do something to help the Mountain Fighters, but I am not sure about the flag," said Flisvos, who had been convinced by Aunt Anna's report. "Besides, who knows what our new flag is supposed to look like?"

"I forgot about that," admitted Philippos. "Aris said that when the enemy's gone we're going to have a brand-new flag."

"Well, so much for the flag," I said.

But Philippos went on talking about it as though

HEADS
OR
TAILS

we all knew it had to be done. He wondered about what the best time of day would be, how to distract the guards, how to climb to the roof of the school building and not be seen. Flisvos and I were agreeing that the danger and the colors and design of our new flag made things difficult.

"Listen, this joke's gone too far," I said in the end. "If they catch us ripping up their flag, they'll skin us alive."

Flisvos and Philippos agreed.

Later in the afternoon the three of us strolled around the schoolyard and watched as a dozen enemy soldiers stood at attention while another lowered their flag.

"I've got it!" said Flisvos.

"What?"

"What?"

"Your grandmother's panties! We'll raise your grandmother's panties instead of our new flag. What do you say?"

Grandmother's panties were old, with patches upon patches of all kinds of colors.

"That's right," said Philippos. "They even have their own string, so there'll be no problem attaching them to the flagpole."

Flisvos had been converted. I kept on opposing the idea silently, hoping that when the time came to pick one of us to climb on the roof, it wouldn't be me.

Philippos ripped a button from his shirt, and looked me straight in the eye. "Heads or tails?" he said.

Three o'clock in the afternoon, when most of the guards are half asleep or playing cards. We'll sneak into the yard of the abandoned house next to the old school building. Philippos had thought it all out. "Take this paper ball with you," he said. "If they catch you, pretend that we were playing, and you went to retrieve the ball." "So far, so good," said Flisvos. And he said, "Climb the pepper tree as high as you can, then hang from the branch that's close to the gutter, then grab the gutter itself—chances are it won't come off." And I said, "Wait a minute." But Philippos had thought it all out. "Don't worry," he said. "Once you've grabbed the gutter, lift yourself up, and go straight to the flagpole." "Yes, but what if the roof tiles slide, or break under my feet?" "See, he's doing it again. All he can think of is disasters," said Flisvos. And Philippos, who had thought it all out, said, "Don't step on the tiles; step in the gutter, and then walk along the spine of the roof that's cemented, you fool." "But what if they catch me after I've ripped down their flag and raised the panties?" "Just don't name names," said Flisvos. And Philippos said, "Play dumb. Like Dando when he was trying to light a cigarette from their trucks' headlights, and the soldiers were laughing, while we were stealing the potatoes in the back." "Maybe we should forget the whole thing," I said. But Philippos and Flisvos said, "Nonsense."

Three o'clock: Most of the soldiers play cards, or sit in their chairs in the shade and lean against the wall, sleepy. Into the yard of the abandoned house next to the school building. Climb the pepper tree, hang from the tall branch that's close to the gutter, then grab the gutter itself. I lift myself up, and walk along the spine of the roof that's cemented, and crawl to the flagpole. At 3:03 I cut the cord and lower the flag of tyranny. Down the flag of tyranny! Up the panties! Yes, but how do you steal Grandmother's only pair of panties? Philippos hadn't thought about that. "Maybe when she takes them off to wash them," said Flisvos. "Aunt Anna washed them for her yesterday," I said. "Besides, Grandmother's sick. It'll be another week or so before the next washday." Philippos hadn't thought about that either. "Maybe we should forget the whole thing," I said. Philippos and Flisvos agreed.

DELIRIA Malaria: the window moves to the ceiling above the bed, a faint pallor, quartered. "The cross," says Grandmother. I take her black scarf, dip it into the bucket, wring it, spread it over my face. The floor moves like the bottom of a boat in rough waters. "Lick the quinine box, it's still bitter," she says. Someone's on the roof, ripping up the flag, then looking down on us through the window. "The cross," says Grandmother. The boat's going to sink. I am cold. Hands and legs shake, teeth chatter. Grandmother says I am dying. My scalp is numb. The shudder creeps up my back to my head, lifts the scalp, hangs it on the door hook. I run my fingers over my head for blood. "My own grandmother was a nun," she says. "When she died, we buried her sitting in her chair, and when we dug her up three years later, she was in fine shape. Her habit was clean, her skin soft and cool, it had a fragrance of wildflowers. . . . Heat water and mix some ashes in it to soften it," she says. "She always put bay leaves and ashes into the water before she washed her hair, and her hair was always soft," she says. A branch thick with dark bay leaves at the window that moved to the ceiling. "Ah, the little red scratch on the lamb's shoulder blade," she says. "Grandma, we haven't had lamb for ages." "Never mind," she says. "When I die, I want to be buried standing. That way the worms will be afraid to come near me." "Grandma, what did the little red scratch say?" " 'Pack up, old woman, pack up.' " "And what did it say about me, Grandmother?" "Don't let them put you flat down there," she says, "or the worms will drill a lot of little holes in your face. When we unburied my own grandmother three years later, her skin had a fragrance of wildflowers." The rocking of the boat. I'm trying to vomit, but all I can get out is a little yellow fluid. "Sit still," she says, "or you'll make me dizzy. And keep talking; it helps to keep the shadows out of this room. Say, who's sitting in that chair by the window?" "I am thinking about a bird's warm, feathery neck." "Not a good sign," she says, "but go on." "My neck is bare like a bald chicken's, and when I shiver, the dirt flakes off and falls into the sea." "Ha!" she says, "that means you won't have to wash your neck with that cold water again. Now let me see those cold little feet. Give me those cold feet and I'll warm them up for you." "I'm down at the bottom of the boat." "That's silly," she says. "What are you doing down there?" "I can't climb up, that's all." "That's not all," she says. "Tell me, who's sitting in that chair in front of the window?"

Once I saw him at the steps of the church, a blind-dumb-and-deaf beggar who had injured his left knee and had preserved that wound with acids to solicit my pity. But when I turned my face the other way, he got hold of his cane from the lower end, and he tried to grab me with its hook.

And once I saw him go from door to door talking to town folk in confidence. The people didn't un-

I
AM
HERE
ONLY
TO
WATCH

derstand him, couldn't see much sense in what he said, but he didn't mind. Yet when I shut the door in his face, he shook his fist and pounded on the door, threatening to come back.

And I saw him counting and counting again his small change, muttering, "Strange, I thought I had more." And when he saw me, he accused me of having stolen his money.

The next time I saw him, it was a sunny winter morning in the deserted square. He squatted in front of a pile of old tires with his fly open, and I thought he was picking lice from his testicles and crushing them between his thumbnails. And then he shook his prick at me, and showed me a handful of change.

Now he's sitting in a chair by the window, waiting, and Grandma says, "He might be a neighbor who's come to help us." Grandmother sleeps with the whites of her eyes showing. Same with the half-eaten gold tooth, every time her wrinkled mouth opens, exhaling. And now he says, "Don't be afraid. I am here only to watch." "Ha!" says Grandmother, opening her eyes. "All this time I thought you were blind."

THE
DEATH
OF
GRANDMOTHER

The window up on the ceiling darkens. I dip the scarf into the water, wring it, and spread it over Grandmother's face. "Not yet," she whispers. "First I am going to put him out of business." "She's going to put you out of your misery," he says, imitating her voice. "That's right," she says. "You tell him don't go out without shoes in this weather or you'll catch a cold, but he goes out anyway, and next thing he's in bed with fever. You tell him don't eat unripe plums, because they'll cut up your insides, but he does anyway, and he gets the runs." "Grandmother, I thought you were talking about him." "So did I," she says. And she says, "Remember my old man's dagger with the three blue dots on its blade? Yes I do," she answers, and she falls asleep.

My eyelids burn. Now and then I shake my head, and the dream stops, only to start again seconds later from the same beginning: I am naked in the dusty square, holding a bunch of grapes. Beside me a rooster with long black and gold plumage leaps into the air, nibbling a grape at a time. As soon as his crooked beak cuts into a grape, I open my eyes, but in a moment I am asleep, and he's at it again. My eyelids burn. I am afraid to sleep. The rooster leaps higher than ever before. He pecks at my neck, plucking a hunk of skin. I open my eyes once again, terrified. His beak, long and rusty, is still cutting into my skin, and I see Grandmother holding the rooster by the neck, which is carved in ivory. His beak is studded with three blue dots. But Grandmother runs out of strength. She makes a deep sound—Aaak!—and the gold tooth shines in the dark of her mouth, then she jerks her head back, and he walks over to her, and he shuts her mouth and eyes.

Cold black fireplace, and thorny little moon caught in the sooty web of the chimney. When I die, I am going to give you my gold tooth, and you won't forget me. But the doors and the windows will be shut forever, and the maps of your illusions will remain unchanged on the stucco of the ceiling. And the floorboards will warp, catapulting their nails into the air. And the table will be empty, and

AND
OVER
THE
EMPTINESS
DUST

165

over the emptiness will be dust. What's shining inside that brandy snifter—a candle? A candle or a tooth. "When I die, I am going to leave this gold tooth for you." "But Grandmother, how are you going to pull it out once you're cold and gone?" "That's a problem," she'd said. And then she'd said, "You'll pull it out." Grandmother knew all about red scratches and bloodstains on the lamb's shoulder blade, and about singing trees, and about herbs that softened the water. "Each time I washed my hair, I cried and called on my mother, whose own hair was raven black like her own mother's." "Why did you cry, Grandmother?" "Soapsuds. Now let me see those icy cold feet of yours. Didn't I tell you not to go out without shoes?" "But Grandmother, I don't have any shoes." "That's one more reason not to go out. Here, I'll unbutton my bosom. Bring me those feet and I'll warm them for you."

Empty the table, and over the emptiness, dust. Over the dust, the habitual searching of your bony fingers. Is it a candle, or a tooth? Whenever I see that glow in the dark, I'll know it's you coming home to visit.

XXV

Following the Sunday Liturgy, four days after Grandmother had been buried, the priest spoke about the coming of Lent. But every time he mentioned the word "Lent," the parishioners, even the most pious of them, looked at each other and grinned. What made that word sound silly was another word: "famine." The priest offered to explain that Lent meant not only moderation with food and drink, but with all kinds of routine or special pleasures that many in his flock indulged in. There were more grins. For a few minutes it seemed that, no matter what the priest said to restore piety, things would get worse and worse. "For nearly two thousand years," he said, "our Lord keeps on suffering on our behalf, and what do you do in return? Lie, fornicate, and revive the most blasphemous pagan customs. On the Sunday before Lent, some of you will again gather in the so-called Sacred Grove to worship the accursed Goat-legged One, and indulge in wine, foul language, and the frenzy of dance and flesh. Can't you see how our Lord punishes us all now for those transgressions? Where is the good food and the intoxicating spirit? Where is the energy for dance, or for . . ." There were smiles and

a few loud laughs. "Yes"—he recovered quickly—
"where, where is the energy to debauch? Do away
with pagan blasphemy, I say, and there may still be
time for your salvation. For if you do not, even
harsher days are ahead for us. And if the Lord
doesn't punish the paganists among you, the authorities will, amen."

The churchgoers left the sermon and the church
that day convinced that the authorities, including
the priest, served the Lord and the Devil with equal
reverence, and they walked home wishing each
other many happy transgressions.

CAPETAN
ANDROMACHE'S
FIRES

The shelling of the mountainside from the town
square had continued for the whole week. The
Mountain Fighters did not answer the challenge.
Even the fires they used to light among the pine
trees disappeared, and we began to worry that the
Fighters had suffered heavy losses. Late that Sunday night I was awakened by what sounded like a
group of neighbors talking excitedly in the street. I
put on my clothes and went to join them. They
were neighbors talking and pointing at the mountainside. What had happened? The little fires had
reappeared among the trees. Flisvos and Philippos
had just gotten out of bed also, and were shivering
in their underwear. "What's going on?"

"My mother says Capetan Andromache probably
heard that we've been worrying about the Mountain Fighters, and decided to let us know that everybody's doing fine up there," said Flisvos.

Then the cannon resounded again from the
square, and someone said, "They're taking aim at
the fires." The small crowd grew silent, and I saw
Flisvos' mother crossing herself.

"I don't understand," she whispered. "I just don't
understand."

As a result of the shelling, the fires began to

spread on the mountainside, burning down the pine trees.

"What's going to happen now?" we asked Flisvos' mother.

"I just can't believe that Capetan Andromache is so simple-minded as to give the swine a target," she said distractedly. "Unless, of course . . ." And her eyes shone suddenly, and she didn't finish her sentence.

"What? What?" insisted Flisvos, pulling her sleeve.

"Never mind," she answered, and, taking Flisvos by the hand, she rushed to her house.

Then my aunt took Philippos by the hand and ran to her house, saying, "You too go home. Get in and lock the door."

Within a minute the street was empty. I went in, locked the door, and watched from the window. When the foot patrol went by, I opened the door and sat on the front steps waiting for Philippos. November curled up on my knees and busied himself licking his fur.

First came Flisvos. "Sh . . . If my mother finds out she'll pluck my ears," he said.

"Did she say what she thought is going to happen?"

"No, but I bet she knows. She just warned me not to even stick my nose out for the rest of the night."

Then Philippos showed up with his slingshot and a pocketful of pebbles. "Well, what's happening?" he asked.

"You tell us," said Flisvos.

"I don't know," whispered Philippos, "but something *is* happening, all right. My mother barred the door and the windows, so I got out through the old barn."

A
NIGHT
OUT

"Well?" said Flisvos.

"Well what?" I said.

"Nothing," said Flisvos.

"Let's go find out what's happening," said Philippos.

"What about the curfew? The patrol might shoot at us."

"We can walk carefully, in the dark," said Flisvos.

I locked the door, and we took a path through alleys and back yards toward the square. Each time the cannon fired, it sounded louder, and the only other sound we could hear was its echo through the ruined houses. It was a moonless night. Halfway to the square I felt something soft moving between my feet, and I jumped toward Philippos, hitting my big toe on a stone. The others got down on their stomachs. Then Philippos stretched out his hand toward me. In his hand he was holding November.

"Here, he's all yours," he whispered.

I took him and put him down. "Go home," I said. I pushed him, kicked him softly, but he didn't move, and as soon as we started to walk, he followed us, meowing. I took him and put him inside my shirt, where he curled up, purring. We stopped behind the old shops on the north side of the square, watching the soldiers who loaded and fired the cannon. Under the white light of a big lamp, we saw the Commandant talk rather casually to Lekas, while the three soldiers worked away, repeating exactly the same movements between two piles of ammunition. They showed neither hurry nor emotion. Their movements were so coordinated with the motion and the sound of the gun that they looked like parts of an automatic device that helped itself to a strange kind of fruit, and then spat out the seeds and rejected the shells.

We tiptoed into a narrow passage between two shops. The smell of old piss was so sharp that November got restless and tried to climb out of my shirt. I slapped him on the head, but instead of stopping he began to claw me and bite me. I took him out, put him down, and stroked his back in order to keep him quiet, but he turned around and bit my toe so hard that I almost screamed. Once he'd taken his revenge, he strolled along the wall, sniffing curiously.

Most of those shops hadn't had toilets, and the night customers of the cafés and the tavernas used to relieve themselves in the alleys behind the shops, or in the narrow spaces between them. The odor was strong. The shopkeepers had to do something about it, and this is what they did: Once a week they paid a kid to go around and paint white crosses on the walls. Would anyone dare piss on a cross? It was a devilish idea, but it didn't work. The crosses were repainted every week, and the piss flowed freely. All of that had come to an end when the enemy confiscated everything and forced the shopkeepers out of business. Since then, the paint of the crosses had turned yellow and had begun to peel off, but the sharp smell of urine was still there.

The cannon had just stopped firing. The Commandant, using his binoculars, was scanning the mountainside, most of which was now in flames. There seemed to be no point in keeping up the shelling. The Commandant lowered his binoculars, then yawned. Afterward he gave brief orders to the cannon crew, and he and Lekas walked the length of the square, chatting. We saw them stop in front of the church, salute one another, then take opposite directions, each returning to his own house. One of the soldiers headed for the old school, leaving the others to guard the cannon. Now and then we could hear the hooting of an owl on the roof of an abandoned house, or the slow, heavy steps of the other two soldiers patrolling the streets. November had disappeared.

SPYING ON LEKAS

The late night breeze brought a fine smell of honeysuckle. The sky was clear, and the stars looked distant. There was no moon. We walked with caution on the new grass, along the dark fences.

Philippos spoke first. "I don't want to go home yet," he said, stopping.

"Let's go and take a peek at the old school," said Flisvos.

"I'd be more interested to see what Lekas is up to now that he's gone back home," said Philippos.

"Up to shooting anything that moves in and around his back yard," I said.

"True, but I've also heard that he's doing some funny things with the red-haired woman he's keeping in his house," said Philippos.

"Like what?" asked Flisvos.

"Oh, I don't know, but I'd like to find out."

"You can't see anything unless you climb up the back-yard wall," I said.

"You don't have to," said Philippos.

"What do you mean?" asked Flisvos.

"Come on, I'll show you. I've figured it all out."

When we got there, Philippos showed us a large eucalyptus tree in a back yard adjacent to Lekas'. He was right. We could climb that tree and look inside Lekas' own back yard, and perhaps his bedroom, through the back window, without getting too close. We reached the tree and looked up to see how thick the foliage was, how well we could hide in it. There was a reflection of light glittering on the fragments of glass that topped Lekas' back-yard wall. That light could only come from his bedroom window. One after another we climbed up into the tree and sat on a branch surrounded by thick foliage. We started to separate the smaller branches that blocked our view of the house. We were so excited and scared that when we whispered to one another our voices trembled. Then Philippos put his finger across his lips. Had he heard something? We stopped moving, breathing. There was a sound of scratching on the bark of the tree. We looked down, but the trunk was hidden behind the leaves of the branch that carried us. The scratching stopped, then started again, followed by a familiar meow.

November couldn't just sit in my lap and relax. He started with Flisvos, jumped onto Philippos' shoulder, lost his balance and fell onto Philippos' legs, which he clawed while trying to regain his balance. "Dumb cat, I'll strangle you," hissed Philippos, but November had already jumped to my lap. I tried to help him relax by stroking his fur, patting his back. No, that wasn't enough, he'd rather climb higher, he'd rather claw my chest and shoulder, claw his way to the top of my head. I couldn't shout to him; I couldn't just lift him and throw him down. If I took both hands off the branch, I'd lose my balance, or make too much noise, or—And November seemed to count on all that, to be taking advantage of my awkward situation. And then he perched on top of my head and busied himself with licking his fur and purring.

We parted the smaller branches once more and looked at Lekas' back window. There was light in the room. Naked figures, one in bed, the other playing around with what seemed to be a small white dog. The cross dividing the window interfered with my view, and I had to keep parting the leaves and moving my head right and left, or up and down, which made the cat lose his balance and claw my

THROUGH
A
RARE
WINDOW

173

scalp. The figure playing with the dog disappeared into another room, and when I looked at the other once again, I knew it was Ermina. I also knew that she wasn't simply lying in bed. Her body seemed to be stretched out, and from the way it moved from time to time, I could tell that her wrists and ankles were tied to the brass posts. Lekas walked into the room, followed by the dog. He went around the bed, stopped by Ermina's feet. He carried something in his left hand that the dog was interested in, as I saw him leap toward it twice. Lekas let the dog sniff that thing, but when the animal reached for it, he raised his hand up high. For the third time the dog tried to get it by jumping at it. Lekas turned around, and, lowering his hand, he rubbed the thing he carried in his hand over the soles of Ermina's feet. Once he had finished, he moved aside, letting the dog have a sniff. The dog then began to lick the soles of Ermina's feet with his long red tongue. Her body began to heave, and her head to rise. She shook her hair back, and I saw her mouth open, I saw her teeth, her lips moving rapidly. She seemed to laugh and at the same time to plead with Lekas. As the dog kept on licking her feet, tickling her, Ermina continued to laugh, but I couldn't hear her voice and I couldn't tell whether she actually laughed or cried.

LAUGHING AND CRYING

November got down from my head, and, after sniffing around for a while, he found a spot of his own on the same branch and closed his eyes. Flisvos kept rubbing his good eye. He said he had trouble seeing through the leaves and wanted to switch places. Philippos looked at the window, stunned.

"I just don't understand why the bastard is wasting that butter on her feet," he muttered.

"How can you tell it's butter?" asked Flisvos.

"What else can it be?"

"I wouldn't want to guess," said Flisvos.

"I mean, if he has to tickle her, why doesn't the shithead do it himself and spare all that butter?"

"Beats me," said Flisvos.

"Look!" I said.

Lekas was back touching Ermina's feet again. If what he held in his hand was a bar of butter, he must have just spread a new layer of it on her soles. The dog went back to work licking it away, and Ermina began to laugh, and to shake violently. Since her wrists and her ankles were tied to the bedposts, she had very little freedom of movement. The convulsions from her laughter forced her body to be stretched out even more as she jerked her stomach and breasts upward, arching her spine. Lekas stood by her side, laughing, only not as uncontrollably as she. The next time she pushed her body upward, Lekas grabbed two pillows and squeezed them under her buttocks. That forced the middle of her body into a permanent arch. Her limbs were so stretched out that she could no longer jolt. And yet as the dog continued to tickle her feet with his tongue, Ermina had no choice but to laugh, immobile except for the small waves of tremor that rippled the surface of her skin, that started from her thighs and rolled upward over her pubic hair, over her stomach, her breasts, her throat, and ended at her teeth, her mouth opening and closing soundlessly.

A cold gust of wind with the damp sharpness of brine from the sea filled our nostrils, passing through the eucalyptus leaves with a rustle, and the skin of our arms and legs shivered. Flisvos' good eye was strained. He began to yawn. I was angry at Lekas. Philippos held his stomach as if he were

THE
TAKEOVER

175

about to throw up. I was curious and angry at the same time. Once again I pushed the leaves aside. This time I saw Lekas holding his prick with both hands and showing Ermina his erection. She was still laughing with convulsions, and for a moment it seemed as if she were laughing at him. Then, as the dog licked her feet, Lekas climbed into bed, and, kneeling between her thighs, he advanced his knees under her, then guided his prick to her crotch. Ermina laughed. Lekas pushed forward. Ermina laughed. Slowly he leaned back, and, stretching out his hands in the same direction, he got hold of her shins. He remained still in that position. He was inside of her, and she laughed. He watched her laugh from a distance. And he watched her body shake, transferring her motion to his. Lekas leaning back, Ermina trembling, working for him through her forced laughter. Then Lekas pushed forward. He moved his body forward and quickly pulled the pillows from under her buttocks. Looser now, Ermina's body began to heave and jolt up and down again, rocking the bed and Lekas himself, who struggled to keep the gap between them closed. He leaned forward, passed his hands under her arms, and, getting hold of her shoulders, he pulled himself up and closer to her, then stretched out his legs alongside of hers. He buried his face between her breasts, kissing and biting them. Clutched firmly to her, Lekas let his entire body follow every movement of hers, like a skillful rider who has just broken in a wild mare. At that moment the night sky was flooded with light. Guided by the sound of an explosion, we looked up and saw a kind of firework that spread like a huge carnation, dyeing everything red in its short-lived radiance. Then we heard rifle shots and machine-gun fire concentrating in several locations throughout the town. The bullets' luminous trajectories showed us that among those locations were the Security Station, the old school building, the square, and the Promontory. It had to be the Mountain Fighters.

A bullet whistled through the leaves. As we started to crawl along our branch toward the center of the tree, we heard the sound of a door opening. We turned around and saw Lekas. He'd just put on a pair of pants and walked through the kitchen door into the yard, holding his rifle. We froze. I thought he'd seen us and was about to start shooting, but then he looked as though he were trying to figure out what all that small arms fire was about. He was surprised, and for a few moments confused. Without losing any more time, he rushed through the yard, and began to climb up the wall. He made it to the top, groaning and cursing as he cut himself against the broken glass that he'd planted there for others. He jumped into the neighboring lot, and we saw him run away from the house, limping, until he disappeared down a dark side street. Ermina, tied hand and foot to the bedposts, still at the mercy of the dog, was still laughing and writhing. As we climbed down the tree, we passed November from hand to hand, dropping him to the ground only when I was halfway down.

Flisvos wanted to go home. Philippos preferred to take a closer look at the fighting. And I thought someone should go into Lekas' house, kick out the dog, and untie Ermina.

"You do that," said Philippos. "I'm going to see what's up."

Flisvos agreed to take November home with him, and after they helped me climb up the wall and jump into the yard, they went their way. I ran, opened the door, heard her cries, turned right, walked into the bedroom. Ermina was no longer laughing, only writhing. The dog had licked her feet clean, but he wouldn't stop; he'd started chewing at her toes and licking the blood. I moved against him, and he growled at me; he showed me his teeth and he growled at me. There was blood on his teeth, he was ready to leap at me, and Ermina said, "There, quick." I opened the drawer and saw a small revolver with a bone handle. I hadn't ever laid hands on one. I never thought a time could come when I might have to fire one. "Quick," said Ermina. I took it, held it with both hands, fired into the dog's mouth. Brain, bone, and blood spattered on the white wall, the rest of the brain pouring from the back of his head as he lay on one side, shaking.

When I untied Ermina's wrists and ankles, I saw how badly her skin had been bruised. Her toes were still bleeding. She was pale. There were two dark crescents under her eyes. As she closed her eyes, her body grew limp and cold. Slowly, she rolled over, face down, and she was still. The bedsheets smelled. They were soiled: sweat, semen, and shit. I pulled the sheets from under her, took them to the bathroom. While she slept, I washed her body with a wet cloth, and covered her with a clean sheet I found in a bathroom cabinet.

Rifle shots, machine-gun barrages, and explosions of hand grenades continued to sound throughout the town for a long time. I put the lights out and sat down, holding the gun. If Lekas came back, I was ready to shoot him in the mouth. I sat down, holding the gun in the dark. It was dark. My hands were shaking. My teeth chattering. I was cold. And then the eucalyptus tree began to sing.

THE
IDEA
OF
DEATH

I was a sparrow and a mouse, and then I was a dog. And the first time I caught myself thinking, I thought, This is something I should be worrying about. Because no one else seemed to be thinking, not the way I was, and the more I thought about thinking, the more I thought and the more I worried.

I was hungry and I hurt, and then I died. And the second time I caught myself thinking, I thought, The way I am thinking about it, it's bound to get worse in the future. Because hunger and pain and death were a way of life, the only life I knew, and if hunger and pain and death would be gone, as everybody said they would, life itself would be gone also.

I was a sparrow, and the first time I died, I caught myself thinking about the idea of death, and the second thing I thought about was death itself, the state of being dead, the state of not being. And I thought, The whole idea about the idea of death is actually the idea of not dying, of escaping death, while the actual state of death is a state of not being, because there is no idea behind it.

And then I was a mouse acrobat, and the second time I died, I died on electric wires, and then I was no longer a mouse, because I no longer was.

And the third time I actually died, I was a dog and had no idea whatever about the idea of death, which is actually the idea of not dying, of escaping death, and the previous deaths were worthless, experiences that had taught me nothing. I didn't remember, I couldn't learn, I didn't know, I couldn't imagine, and at the same time there was something terrible that I couldn't forget. I sat in the dark, holding the gun I had just fired; and in the dark I heard my hind legs twitch as the brain unfolded from my skull onto the floor, steaming. I sat in the dark, waiting. I was voiceless. My only defense in the dark was my shivering.

I heard steps around the house, and I stood up, holding the revolver with both hands. Someone broke the lock and kicked the main door in. Others began to knock on the shutters with rifle butts.

IS
THE
WAR
OVER?

"Lekas, surrender!" It was a woman's voice coming from the main door.

"Come out with your hands up!" A man's voice, following a pounding on the bedroom window.

As I approached the main door, I saw the woman's figure against the pink light of dawn. She wore heavy shoes, trousers, army fatigues crossed with cartridge belts, and a worker's cap. She carried a Marsip automatic under her arm. She was a small woman.

"Where's that dog?" she asked when I got close.

I showed her my gun. "I blew out his brains," I said.

"What? You killed Lekas?"

"Yes. I saw his brains pour onto the floor, and his legs twitching."

Several Mountain Fighters who had taken up positions around the house now gathered in front of the door, and I recognized my Uncle Iasson among them.

"We've been looking for you," he said, embracing me and lifting me up. "Are you all right?"

"She's alive," I said, giving him my gun, "but she might need a doctor and medicine." And I said, "Where's my father? Is my father all right? Did we beat the enemy? Did we win the war? Is the war all over?"

LIBERATION By sunrise, the Mountain Fighters were everywhere. Many enemy soldiers and informers had been killed in the fighting, and the rest of them, including the Commandant, had been captured.

When the sun came out, Capetan Andromache herself climbed up the church tower and rang the big bell. Doors and windows began to open. Several people had already gathered in the square, disbelieving, overcome with joy, then frightened again at the thought of the enemy sending more troops to punish the town.

"It's possible," said Capetan Andromache. "Other bands have taken over all the neighboring villages, but the swine might not be ready to run."

"Well, aren't you going to chase them?" yelled an old toothless woman in the crowd.

"Sure we'll chase them. But we're still outnumbered. And the Allies haven't shown up yet. They said they'd send help. 'Go ahead,' they said, 'attack, and we'll be there.' . . . They're still on the way."

"Chase them, chase them," insisted the old woman.

"We'll chase them, but we need help," said Capetan Andromache. "Are you going to give us a hand?"

"Any time," said the old woman, shaking her walking stick.

"What about food?" asked Philippos, who had been around the square even before the fighting ended.

"We'll open the school," said Capetan Andromache, smiling. And she said, "If you promise to go to school, we'll open it for you."

"Yes, yes," shouted everybody.

"We'll open the school and share all there is," said Capetan Andromache, but I am sure that food won't last forever. You must now go back to your fields and plant them for the summer."

"Yes, yes."

"What about Lekas? What about that snake?" asked Tryfos from the crowd.

"He can't be far. We must find him and plant him too," said Capetan Andromache.

A dozen Mountain Fighters led by Capetan Andromache opened up the old school and handed out all of the enemy's provisions: grain, oil, canned food, and clothing. I stood in the line with Flisvos and Philippos, each one of us holding a small basket, and when our turn came to get our share, it was my cousin Aris who decided what we should be given. He sat at a little desk keeping a record of everything on a sheet of paper which he held down with the wrist of his writing hand. His left arm was no longer there. He wore a black band around his folded, pinned sleeve, and when I asked him if that was his mourning for Grandmother's death, he said no, that was his mourning for the loss of his arm.

XXVI

Later that day, Old Petros showed up in the square, and Tryfos approached him, asking if he had heard anything about Lekas.

AGENT R. (16–21)

"No," said Old Petros, "but I've got more news about our friend R."

"Never mind," said Tryfos.

"Listen, that story is getting interesting."

"Which story?" asked a newcomer.

Once again, Old Petros was surrounded by a small audience.

"The true story of R.," explained Kyr Notis, rolling his eyes.

"Who's R.?" asked the newcomer.

"Listen, and you might figure it out," said Old Petros. And he said, "Where was I? Ah, yes, paragraph sixteen." And he went on with the story:

16. R. received orders from the Allied Command to coordinate plans with the Mountain Fighters for a general assault on the enemy. In addition, R. received a coded message which he was ordered to pass on to Capetan Andromache.

17. Capetan Andromache deciphered the mes-

sage. It said, "Proceed with operation Korax as planned. Allied support by air and sea imminent." And it said, "Agent R. known collaborator. Repeat: Agent R. dangerous. Liquidate promptly."

18. Capetan Andromache burned the message, and told R. nothing about its contents. She only advised him to quit the war effort as an agent of the Allies, and join the Mountain Fighters or go home, because the Allies' ideology is changing—whatever that means, she said.

19. R. thanked Capetan Andromache and returned to headquarters in E. to report on his mission. In the meantime the relations between the Allies and the Mountain Fighters throughout the country had soured, and R. was once again arrested, this time for high treason.

20. R. was court-martialed and his former radio operator was brought to testify that he, R., had in fact collaborated with the Mountain Fighters, not once but twice.

21. R. was sentenced to be hanged by the neck until he was dead, and then his previous suspended sentence was revoked, so he received another death sentence, or a sentence to be hanged twice by the neck until he was dead, or until he was dead twice, or . . .

"Hey, wait a minute. What's your hurry anyway?" said Old Petros as his listeners began to drift away. "Don't you want the rest of it? Aren't you interested to hear what happened next? . . ."

On the third day after the liberation of our town, Capetan Andromache and her army returned to the mountain for an assembly of resistance groups from all over the country. They took the hostages along. Six fighters, including Aris, stayed on as the town's new garrison.

We began to plow the fields, hoping that it wasn't too late in the season to expect a good wheat harvest. Aunt Anna found a bag full of old watermelon seeds, and she handed them out in the square, saying, "If all of them sprout we'll have enough watermelons to feed an army." And Tryfos said, "We're no longer slaves of the enemy; we can go back to being slaves of the earth."

The last Sunday before Lent arrived with tambourine, double-flute, and bell sounds. When we woke up in the morning, the Priapic Criers were already out in the streets wearing animal masks and two-foot-long phalluses with springs, which they jumped at the women like jacks-in-the-box, singing songs such as "The Jackass's Fifth Leg," "The Widow's Thirsty Garden," and "Ramming the Virgin's Gate." In between songs, they urged people to indulge in transgressions, and indulge now, suggesting unusual ways of doing it, depending on the weather, the age and the size of the partners, or the family history. Folks would send the children indoors and laugh heartily, or talk back to the Criers, recommending funnier positions. Older men would grin under their thick mustaches or shake their walking sticks, while their old ladies would pretend to be outraged, plugging their ears. When the Criers reached the crossroads, they stopped and read passages from an old hand-written book which was called *Antigospel*. The language of that book was so formal that I could make out only a few words like "cunticle," "penissimo," "posterior hemispheres," and such. They ended each passage with a prolonged "Amen." As they moved on through the neighborhoods, they urged any unmarried adults they came across not to miss the "Synod," otherwise known as the "Usual Annual," which was to take place that night at the Sacred Grove, a tiny island in the river.

THE
ANCIENT
RITES
BEGIN

According to a legend, the Sacred Grove used to be a sanctuary dedicated to the Goat-legged One and the Nymphs. In the old times the sanctuary had a priestess, and a marble statue of the God seated, with a glorious erection. Once a year the women who ran the town locked up the men in the houses, then took all the young virgins to the God in a colorful procession of torchlights. The virgins undressed and sat one after another in the God's lap. Virginity was then too sacred a thing for mortal men to tamper with. But later in the night, once the God had been honored, the men were set free and allowed to join in the festivities. Time passed and Christianity invaded the town and the island, and the first Christian priest took a little hammer and made a perfectly smooth seat of the God's lap. Everybody thought Christianity would come up with a god or saint of its own for a similar ritual, but it didn't, so our people preserved the old one. Since then, the rules of the festival have changed, and the men have refused to be excluded from the first part of it.

Philippos, Flisvos, and I were not old enough to be allowed on the island, so we arrived early and hid in a raspberry thicket. When the moon came out, the young men and women of our town began to show up one or two at a time, dressed in costumes and wearing masks. Some of them were already trying to recognize one another, which was cheating, but as Philippos said, Who wants an unpleasant surprise? There was no wine. The flasks that several men had brought in were filled with "quick brew," a kind of beer made from oats. As the crowd increased, we saw a group of newcomers lighting a small fire with fragrant weeds and dried roots. They sat around inhaling the smoke with bamboo flutes, then playing music with them. They were joined by guitar and tambourine players. When the dance started, four men dragged the small bridge over onto the island so that no one would leave before dawn. The crowd cheered. More and more people were joining hands to dance, and the single file moved rhythmically among the old trees, then around the fire and the musicians. Then Philippos recognized Aris among the dancers. Since his brother had only one arm, he could dance only at the end of the line. But Philippos couldn't tell whether or not the woman who danced next to Aris was Lemonia.

Then Flisvos got excited and he almost forgot that we were hiding: "Look!"

"Look," he whispered again.

"What? What?"

"The woman wearing the green mask."

"Where?"

"In the middle of the line. She's also wearing a hat, but her hair's showing."

She was taller than the other women, and she danced so gracefully that the man who followed her in the line was losing his steps.

"Yes, I see her hair," I said. The man who followed her, losing his steps, was Uncle Iasson.

THE FIRE DANCE

When the musicians join the dance, who is to play the music? The dancers slowed down, started to talk to each other, and we were afraid that the whole thing might degenerate into a dull party. But within two minutes we heard a lovely clear voice filling the night. It was Ermina. She sang the first two lines of an old love song, followed by the others, who repeated the words while dancing. Ermina's voice sounded again, singing the next two lines. Philippos, Flisvos, and I, tired of our hiding, came out of the thicket and sang with the chorus from a distance. There were more songs, but the line soon broke, as the men and women now preferred to dance in twos. When the moon began to lean toward the western sky, and most of the ground was filled with shadows of trees, Uncle Iasson spread the lighted roots and sticks of the fire, and he asked the dancers to take their shoes off. They did, and the traditional fire dance was under way, to the rhythm of bamboo flutes and clapping hands. The tempo of the music increased. The dancers jumped faster and faster while singing or laughing, or screaming when a lit coal got stuck between their toes. A few men took their shirts off. A few women got rid of their blouses. Shoulders, breasts, stomachs, and backs glistened in their sweat, but the stomping on the fire raised a cloud of ashes, and more dancers hurried to get rid of their clothes, keeping only their masks on. We moved closer. The dance was approaching its peak, and we saw that many men had erections. That added a new feature to the dance. When the dancers jumped up and down facing one another, the men also moved forward, which made the women turn to the side gently and laugh. Trousers, skirts, and underwear flew off at every turn of the music, in every direction. Although the masks were kept on, by that time we could recognize most of the dancers. One of them was Lemonia.

"Paganists! Satanists!" resounded the priest as he sprang out of the bushes, his black cassock flying behind him. He rushed furiously forward, holding what seemed to be the Bible in his left hand, and a horsewhip in his right. "Repent, ye children of Baal," he shouted, cracking his whip in the air before bringing it down on the bare backs, breasts, buttocks, and erections of the dancers.

We were stunned. Aris took Lemonia by the hand and ran into the bushes. Other than that, the priest's raid hardly disturbed the dance. On the contrary, as he strode about striking right and left, he seemed to be himself a part of it. Now the dancers held on to each other even tighter, stepping aside only when the whip came down hissing in their direction, but some didn't even bother to do that. They kept jumping around the priest, a whirlwind of laughter, rhythm, and dust, until he exhausted himself and seemed to be getting dizzy.

"Lord, release the heavens' cataracts and dispatch the fury of your floods against the sinners!" he shouted at the end, raising his eyes, the whip, and the Bible toward the starry sky. And when he'd finished, four of the dancers grabbed him by the arms and legs, and, chanting the hymn of baptism, they took him to the bank, and one-two-three, they threw him into the water—splash and Amen.

A few more couples ran into the bushes holding hands. Philippos, Flisvos, and I crawled back into the raspberry thicket, but we soon heard voices nearby. We decided to move on. We stopped.

"Sh . . ."

ARIS
AND
LEMONIA

"Where?"

"I think it's Aris and Lemonia," whispered Philippos.

They lay on the grass naked, kissing. Their limbs shone in the moonlight, and there was a smell of sweat and a smell of ashes in the air. Aris whispered something, but we couldn't hear his words. Lemonia held his face to her breast, panting, and Philippos said, "Sh . . ."

"What?" said Flisvos.

"Don't look," said Philippos.

"I can't help it."

Lemonia rolled onto her back, and Aris was on top of her, parting her legs. He leaned forward, but then he couldn't touch her, as he had to use his only hand to support his weight. We saw him balancing, then lowering his body to cover hers.

"Come on, don't look," said Philippos.

"Sh . . ." said Flisvos.

Lemonia held Aris' weight, embracing him. Slowly he put his hand between her thighs and at the same time he pulled the lower part of his body closer to hers. Lemonia began to raise her legs, and we saw Aris' hand move up and down gently, touching her, rubbing against her. Lemonia turned her face, resting her cheek on her shoulder. She closed her eyes, and we heard her voice whispering, "Yes." She closed her eyes, and he pulled his hand out and moved forward, but before he could stretch out his hand against the ground, he lost his balance and fell onto his left side. Aris lay on his side silent, still. Lemonia turned to her right side, facing him. She began to stroke his hair and to weep. "Come," she whispered with trembling voice, pulling herself closer. Aris turned his face down, pressed it against the grass. "Come, hold me again," she whispered. Then she moved onto her left side and pulled Aris' hand over her breast. Aris lifted his face and began to kiss the back of her neck. Slowly he lowered his hand over her hip, and drew himself closer, pressing against her buttocks, hiding her entire body from us. All we could see then was the back of Aris' body as it moved and shook gently, pressing steadily into her.

The number of the dancers was getting smaller and smaller as the young couples continued to disappear, looking for grassy spots or patches of moonlight among the trees. When the cooler breeze of dawn crept over the river, wrinkling the surface of the water, the Grove was still filled with the pleasant odor of sweating bodies. Philippos, Flisvos, and I strolled among the old trees cautiously, looking for Ermina and Uncle Iasson. We saw them standing next to a tree, kissing, Uncle Iasson embracing Ermina and the tree together. We sat down at a distance, watching, but soon we heard a noise in the bushes nearby, and we ducked. When I looked again, I saw the masked face of a man disappear behind the foliage. Uncle Iasson let go of the tree, and at that moment Ermina shook her long red hair and looked at the moon. Then I heard a long, long cry that sounded like the end of a song sung by the tree that Ermina leaned against, but Philippos and Flisvos thought it was Ermina herself singing. Uncle Iasson took her in his arms, spun her twice, and laid her down by the root of the tree, laughing, and he wiped her eyes as if there were tears in them.

"Why is she crying?" asked Flisvos.

"Sh . . ."

"Maybe she's had too much," said Philippos.

"Too much of what?"

"Sh . . ."

Uncle Iasson touched Ermina's lips with his fingertips. He touched her again with lips and fingers, tracing the moonlight among the shadows of the

IASSON
AND
ERMINA

leaves on her skin, which made her stretch out her arms and legs, shuddering. Then she parted her lips, and her teeth seemed to sink into the soft flesh of the moon, a bitter lemon that made her mouth water. Ermina's nipples grew hard, the muscles of her stomach twitched, twice they twitched. . . . It had happened to Grandmother once; something or other had amazed her. "Well, I left my mouth open and guess what happened, a butterfly flew right in, kept fluttering in my stomach, tickling me, fluttering its wings and tickling me." Grandmother had to swallow a spoonful of kerosene to recover.

"Sh . . ."

"What?"

"Look."

Uncle Iasson was kissing Ermina's stomach. He pushed against the ground with both hands, slid down, kissed the muscles of her thighs, he held her hands down in the moist grass, pressed his face between her thighs, his mouth into her crotch. And right behind them, half-lit, half-shaded by the moon through the leaves, I saw once more the masked face staring at the two lovers and growling.

Quickly Ermina pulled her hands out of the grass, away from his, and, stretching them back, she embraced the tree which then let out a cry like the end of a song, and I saw her stomach twitch six-seven more times.

They lay side by side, panting, then kissing again, both faces hidden in her hair, arms moving over arms, legs already entwined, their motion slow and changing. They rolled from back to back, then lay still for a moment to listen to the soft reverberation of the grass unbending. I lowered my head and saw the moon setting behind the ridge of Uncle Iasson's back, and as she held him to her breast, the moon slipped down between her hands and she missed it. Ermina moved her hands to his loins, over the bones of his hips, pulling him closer, pushing herself against him. She was impatient. I saw her turn her face right and left, slapping her cheeks against the grass. Ermina raised her legs over his shoulders, and rapidly he closed the gap between them, hiding from me the violet shade at the ends of her thighs. They held each other's faces, and looked into each other's eyes and strained expressions, and when they recognized that strain, they both smiled, a strained smile that disrupted their motion and changed it.

The masked face looked down, and when it looked their way again I saw the barrel of a rifle next to it. I saw the rifle rising, taking aim, and I jumped to my feet, shouting, It's Lekas! I think it's Lekas! Uncle, Ermina take cover, he'll kill you! I tried to shout, but there was no sound coming out of my mouth. I tried again, felt the corners of my mouth splitting, but the two lovers couldn't hear me. They kept on moving up and down, turning and rolling on their backs, and the mouth of the rifle followed each move closely, the partner of the loudest sigh.

They stopped, held fast in each other's arms, held their breath, held their eyes closed. Nothing that can't be seen can exist right now—hold fast— you and I and the fall of the earth. The weapon had stopped when they stopped, and I knew it would fire. It fired. I jumped out, ran, tried to cover them with my body—Bam! Too small, my body half the size of theirs—Bam! I pushed them, they wouldn't part, I pushed again—Bam! We tumbled. Sweating muscles and a taste of ash. I tried to stay on top of them, but we tumbled—Bam! Bam! Blood, and a jolt, salty blood and sweat and a smell of burnt leaves.

We stopped, held fast to one another with hands and legs, held our breath, kept our eyes shut, unable to tell who saw the fall of the sky and who the end of the world. We heard steps, more steps, people running, we heard screams and the sound of fists thudding onto bare flesh. Steps again, then the crackling of branches, a voice saying, "Pull off his mask!" Wrestling bodies and a crackling of branches, and, "Aaaah!" And another voice shouting, "It's Lekas, the swine, the jackal!" He fought to free himself, they hit him, his voice crying out, "She's mine, she belongs to me." More sounds of beating fists and the crackling of branches—the breaking of bones and the pulling apart of his limbs.

Blood, then a smell of sweat, then a taste of ashes. And the three of us down, still down, embraced in a tangle, holding our breath, unable to move, afraid to move.

We held our breath and started to get cold, so that none of us would notice any difference in the others. Still down, motionless, a tangle getting cold, hoping that others too wouldn't ever wish to find out for themselves and begin to pull us apart, sorting out who's dead and who's afraid.

XXVII

Most of the fields had been planted. As the days became longer and the vegetable season drew near, many families prepared to move to the country for night work. The Mountain Fighters were freeing town after town, pushing north, but large units of enemy forces were still behind the lines, and the Allies praised our courage but sent no help.

One afternoon, a convoy of enemy tanks and trucks full of soldiers crossed our town on its way north, but word came that the Mountain Fighters had blown up a bridge on the highway, and the enemy commander ordered the convoy to stay on. Then he ordered the reoccupation of the school building and the Security Station, and the eviction of twenty families from their homes in order to provide accommodations for his staff. Aris and the other fighters fled to the mountain, where they rejoined Capetan Andromache. Two days later, Aris came back secretly to let us know that the Mountain Fighters did not plan to attack the convoy while it was stationed in our town. The enemy commander sent a crew to repair the bridge. It was a period of uneasiness and impatience for everyone,

THE
ENEMY
RETURNS

especially the enemy. The soldiers didn't show much interest in our affairs. They busied themselves mostly with housework: washing and mending their uniforms, polishing their boots, inspecting and repairing truck engines, replacing tires. Most of their provisions were kept in the trucks. They baked their bread in the town bakery and cooked dried vegetables. They had brought with them several dozen calves, which they kept in the schoolyard, slaughtering two or three of them each day for fresh meat. They fed the calves with the same dried vegetables that they themselves ate instead of salad.

Word went around finally that the bridge was ready, and the Mountain Fighters were engaged in battle in another area. The convoy rattled northward, raising clouds of dust. Then we saw five soldiers looking for one of their officers who, they said, had disappeared. They went around shouting, "Lalo, Lalo," which we thought was the name of the missing officer, but they didn't find him, and at the end of the day they got in the last truck and drove north to catch up with the others.

The convoy didn't get very far. Capetan Andromache blew up the bridge once more, splitting the enemy force in two, then attacking it on both sides of the river.

THE
COLLECTOR
OF
OLD
DEBTS

The Mountain Fighters came back to distribute most of the food and the calves they'd captured, and once again they withdrew onto the mountain, leaving behind only a six-man garrison and a schoolteacher. Before we knew it, Philippos, Flisvos, and I found ourselves in a classroom in the old school, trying to remember what we did in the last meeting several years before.

By the time the Allies finally arrived, the Mountain Fighters had already beaten or chased the enemy all the way to the borders. The Allies spoke with admiration about the spirit of our people, and sent in representatives to decorate our fighters with medals and titles. Those representatives were also authorized to negotiate economic aid, and to give us expert advice about our future government. By July, most of our fighters had given up their arms to help with the harvest, or had gone back to fishing, weaving, shoemaking, and other trades. Then the first crops of wheat, vegetables, and fruit began to appear, but as there was still no money around, all transactions were done on exchange. People didn't seem to mind that. The Allies objected. "You need to have money," they said. "Nothing can be done right without money," they said. And they said, "You have to have financial aid, if only to be able to pay your old debts. But who's going to give you financial aid if you don't have a responsible government?" they asked. First things first, we needed a responsible government.

When the Mountain Leaders got together to talk about the future, Capetan Andromache said that we shouldn't repeat the mistakes of the past, and that we should let the people of our country take time to think before making a decision. As for the old debts, she said, let the Allies send the collector.

They did. The Allies sent the collector of old debts. He was an admiral. He arrived in a warship followed by enough other warships to fill every port in the country. "See?" he seemed to say in a newspaper photo that showed him holding a document and smiling. In another photo there was the magnified document alone, showing the figures of the money we owed. Long figures of millions and billions. All the other photos showed the warships.

Our leaders met again and decided to negotiate with the Allies. There were arguments among them, and arguments between them and the Allies. The negotiations broke down and started again.

The newspapers were full of articles about what the Allies had to say, but somehow our leaders didn't say much, and when the papers quoted them, they only seemed to be asking questions.

I returned to my shadow theater. I took the photograph of the collector of old debts and copied it on cardboard, making a new puppet.

THE
WATERMELON
INCIDENT

Right at the peak of the watermelon season, the Allies dispatched a military band to our town to play in celebration of the harvest. The musicians were given the old school to spend the night in, but instead of leaving the next day, they stayed on, doing military maneuvers. We began to worry. We told them that hospitality had limits, but they laughed at us. They said, "We don't trust you, the way you eat watermelon, so we've decided to stay awhile and keep an eye on you."

We already knew that the Allies were appalled at the way we ate watermelon and spat out the seeds, so we thought there might be a hidden meaning in their words. We used watermelon eating to protest their presence. We gathered outside the school with big slices of watermelon, which we ate aggressively, and spat out the seeds in the schoolyard toward the soldiers. They hated it. The next day we went back. They shook their fists at us, but we didn't leave. We kept eating slice after slice and spitting out the seeds at them. On the third day, we saw them getting into their truck, and we thought they were leaving. Not so. They drove all over town and out to the fields, confiscating at gunpoint the entire watermelon crop, then piling it up into three neatly stacked pyramids in the town square. What now? We watched. Their chief officer, the conductor, ordered two of his men to guard the watermelons day and night. No one was supposed to have any without permission. Our watermelons! What next? We sent Aris to the mountain to talk to Capetan Andromache about it. She sent word back advising us to remain calm. "The Allies are up to something dirty," she said, "and they might be looking for an opportunity to start messing around. Don't give them that opportunity."

Then the chief officer, the conductor, came to the square and sat at a little table. We were invited to approach and watch. He showed us a knife and a fork. Knife in the right hand, fork in the left. He sliced a watermelon. Removed the first slice. Pinned down the slice with the fork. Cut a small chunk. Pinned it down with the fork, and pitted it with the tip of the knife. Removed the chunk from the slice with the fork, ate it, and invited us to do the same. If we could do it well and in that civilized manner, we could have as much as we pleased. We began to make fun of him by imitating, then exaggerating the way he handled knife and fork, and the way he ate. Then we began to worry again. The sun was hot, and we were thirsty. It was torture seeing the conductor crush chunk after chunk of watermelon between his teeth, while we were so thirsty and yearned for it. And then we began to worry about the fate of the whole harvest. The conductor quit for the night, but the guards stayed on. We organized a watermelon vigil. We spent the night and the next morning around the conductor and the watermelons, protesting.

During the vigil, we told watermelon stories to pass the time. Some of them were real-life stories, others were made up on the spot to fit the occasion and boost our morale. The Allies boosted theirs with the arrival of a small tank to join their ongoing military maneuvers. That tipped the balance even more in their favor, and we decided to call on Barba-Rotas as a last resort. "Sure," he said.

BARBA-
ROTAS

Barba-Rotas had a reputation for having the worst evil eye in town. He'd made a lot of people sick, especially children, when he praised their beauty and physical health. When he was young, he'd made a certain adversary impotent, and a lovely wealthy woman faint into his arms. He had a knack for disasters. He had caused droughts, floods, meals to go bad in the pot while cooking. "Sure," he said, "I'll be more than happy to help." But Barba-Rotas could also cause disasters without meaning to, and many people avoided talking to him, afraid that his eye might close in on them. As a result, he was a lonely and remorseful person. To lessen the chances of causing grief unwillingly, he wore a pair of dark sunglasses at all times. "Sure," he said, "I'll do anything for the community."

When he showed up in the square and took off his sunglasses, the crowd got out of his way so fast that the conductor became alarmed and reached for his revolver.

Barba-Rotas sat in a chair and smiled at him. "I see you're a handsome, healthy-looking young man, which is fine with me," he said.

We shuddered. The conductor went back to his watermelon, smiling.

"That's right," said Barba-Rotas staring at him. "You sure are in top shape, my boy. And look at those pretty blue eyes and blond hair. . . . If this were wheat instead of watermelons, I wouldn't be able to tell you apart. I bet you take after your mother, don't you?" Barba-Rotas kept staring at him.

The conductor did not understand, but he seemed to find the old man amusing. He smiled, stared back at him, had another piece of watermelon, smiled, turned around to look at the two guards who stood behind him, smiled, looked at the crowd, looked at Barba-Rotas questioningly, blushed, tasted another chunk of watermelon, smiled, covered his mouth with the palm of his hand, turned around, and began to vomit.

We applauded Barba-Rotas' performance, cheered, but he raised his hand, and we quieted down. He was trying to focus on the first pyramid of watermelons.

The conductor was throwing up so violently that the two guards had to hold him by the arms to keep him from falling.

"Crack," said Barba-Rotas. Nothing happened. "Crack," he said once again. Nothing. "Explode!" he shouted, and a large watermelon at the base of the first pyramid blew up as if it were filled with compressed air, causing the neat construction to collapse.

The guards quickly dragged their sick officer out of the way of the rolling watermelons. We cheered Barba-Rotas wildly.

He raised his hand again: another explosion, and the second pyramid came down.

The guards panicked, let their officer fall. Unable to protect the watermelons, they started to fire their rifles in the air.

"Explode!" ordered Barba-Rotas. The third pyramid tumbled down.

"Let's gather our good watermelons," yelled Aunt Anna.

We went to work chasing the watermelons, putting them back together into small groups. Barba-Rotas put his sunglasses on, smiling with satisfaction. For the first time in his life he'd done something for which the whole town was grateful. But the joy didn't last. He'd hardly put his sunglasses on, when we heard him shout, "The tank, the tank."

We heard the metallic rattle, and saw the tank rolling toward us at full speed. We thought we were about to be machine-gunned. We ran to take cover behind the shops. The tank ran over the watermelons, turning them into pulp. It went back and forth and in circles, crushing every single watermelon, and the town square looked like a battlefield strewn with corpses wearing green uniforms, strewn with raw flesh, stained with red patches of blood.

XXVIII

The next time the negotiations between the Allies and the Mountain Leaders broke down, the newspapers quoted the Allies as using the word "impasse." Most of us hadn't heard that word before, but everybody started using it right away. Since most of the people used it for the sake of novelty without knowing what it meant, the Allies dispatched speakers throughout the country explaining not only the meaning and the history of the word, but also the context in which it had been used and the substance of the argument behind the interruption of the negotiations. The speakers went on to say that among the Mountain Leaders there was a minority of radical or impractical opinion, represented by Capetan Andromache and a few others. "Not that we doubt their patriotism and their intentions," said the speakers; "but it so happens that Capetan Andromache and Company are simple, uneducated, inexperienced, and too stubborn to see our position or read the signs of the times." Although everybody heard the speakers themselves, the newspapers published the entire speech anyway, and in their next edition they carried the news of Capetan Andromache's assassination.

WE
ONLY
WISH
TO
HELP

The Allies paid tribute to Capetan Andromache and sent a representative to her funeral. During his brief eulogy, he spoke about the deep sorrow of the Allies over the untimely end of our outspoken leader's career. They and every decent human being in the world deplored this thoughtless act of violence, he said, and on behalf of the Allies he offered expert investigative assistance in finding the assassin and unmasking the conspiracy, if there had been a conspiracy.

Three days after Capetan Andromache's funeral, the negotiations started over, and some of the Mountain Leaders were quoted in the papers as having said that we had made mistakes. The Allies did not show any hard feelings. They only said that we should go ahead and form a temporary government, and they promised that some of the cabinet posts would be given to Mountain Leaders, subject again to negotiation, and depending on qualifications. The negotiations broke down for another week, during which an ex-informer fired three shots, wounding one of Capetan Andromache's close associates who acted as the spokesman for our region. The informer was caught and interrogated. He confessed that he'd been paid to kill, but did not know who had given him the gold. Once again the Allies deplored the incident, and offered a reward for information leading to the arrest and final conviction of any members of a conspiracy, if that were the case.

The negotiations resumed, with further promises, suggestions, and threats in the form of friendly visits by foreign dignitaries and naval units. The Allies were saying that they were also anxious about the reorganization of our army, and although some of our representatives said we were not ready to organize or reorganize our army, as a matter of fact we were not at all sure whether or not we wanted to have an army, the Allies went ahead and sent their military experts anyway. They also sent experts to reorganize the courts and establish a number of philanthropic institutions. That did it. Our representatives pulled out of the negotiations once more, saying, "We did not put up with enemies; we won't put up with so-called Allies." The problem was, the Allies already knew that most of the Mountain Fighters had broken their rifles and gone to work. In our region there were only about a hundred of them left. During the day, they were out in the fields helping the farmers with the harvest, and in the night they camped on the mountain, lighting little fires as they did in the war.

Our representatives pulled out of the negotiations for good, saying that only our people had the right to decide about the future of our country. And the Allies said, "We only wish to help." There were more assassinations, but the Mountain Leaders never returned to bargain, and a week or so later, a squadron of unidentified planes flew low over our town from the south and bombed the mountain, and when the sun came out in the morning all the Mountain Fighters were dead, and the mountainside itself looked like a vast quarry.

That summer, we saw our hopes for freedom diminish. We had won the war, but it seemed as if we had lost our country. If we cared for our lives, we could not afford to look into our lives. Instead, we had to pay attention to others who were powerful, for our lives depended on their decisions. If we cared for our town, we could not afford to look into its affairs. Instead, we had to keep up with what went on in the capitals of the world, for the fate of our town depended on the outcome of their affairs.

We began to speak the language of newspapers. Not that we always understood the news and the articles we read. The radio explained what the papers said, but often we didn't even understand the explanations. That distant world that had robbed our attention was too vast to resist, and too elusive to grasp. We waited for the news: the arrival of the dailies, and the radio bulletins. If things went a certain way out there, we were in good shape. If things went another way, we were crushed.

We did not neglect our lives completely. Philippos, Flisvos, and I continued to spend a lot of time together, but what we did, or talked about, was less and less fun. Philippos also spent some time helping Lemonia with housework as the wedding day drew near. Lemonia was pregnant since the last Sunday before Lent, and her father the priest had finally yielded to her engagement with Aris. And I often kept company with Ermina, who had gone through a second operation to have Lekas' bullets removed from her neck and shoulder. She and Uncle Iasson were making plans to live together after she had recovered from her wounds. For a while, Flisvos was obsessed with a news item about research done abroad to help the millions of people who had been maimed in the war. "Banks" was the word. Banks for spare human parts, real as well as artificial, which could be transplanted or attached to make up for the lost ones. In Flisvos' case, it would be only a matter of choice: he could have a real eye from a donor who'd just died in an accident, or an electric one, which was preferable. "You don't even have to wear it in your socket all the time," he said, "and it can see in the dark. If you're looking for something in your pocket, you can actually *look* there by putting it inside your pocket," he said. "And if you have a toothache, you can put your eye in your mouth and actually see which tooth has a cavity. Or," he said, "you can leave it at home and see everything that's going on there while you're away."

INVASION OF STRANGERS

Once in a while there were rumors and newspaper reports that the prisoners of war and other hostages who had been held in enemy camps had been freed and were on their way home. One morning Flisvos came to tell me that, after all, my mother was one of them. I didn't believe it and didn't think about it anymore, but all of a sudden, all kinds of strange-looking people started showing up in the fields, and we were afraid that our town was about to be invaded by hungry men and women from another part of the country. They were thin, pale, with a layer of dust all over their hair and clothes. We went into our houses, double-locked the doors, and watched from behind the window curtains. The strangers kept knocking on our doors, mentioning the names of the missing and of those who had been in enemy camps abroad. One by one the doors began to open, but the strangers pretended that they were the prisoners and exiles. We asked them certain questions, hard questions, to prove that they were impostors, but somehow they kept coming up with the right answers. We did not recognize them. We refused to pretend that we recognized them. Some of them were allowed to come in, but we were never convinced that they were the real missing ones.

The woman who insisted that she was my mother made herself at home and began to take care of the house as though it were hers. She cleaned the chimney, painted the kitchen, washed the floorboards and the windows, even my clothes; and little by little, first she complained about my shadow theater, then brooded about Flisvos and Philippos, and how they distracted me from other things I ought to be doing. I put my shadow theater puppets in the basket and went to my grandfather's to ask him if I could move in, but he sent me right back, saying, "Chances are that woman is indeed your mother, and you should listen to what she has to say, because it's all for the best." When I went back, she took the basket from my hands and threw my puppets into the fireplace and burnt them.

THE ERA OF PEACE AND RECON- STRUCTION

We brought down the bodies of the Mountain Fighters to give them a proper burial, but there was no room in the cemetery for all of them. We didn't know what to do. We took them back to the mountain, buried them among the scorched pine trees. That day the teacher said, "There will be no classes today." And he said, "There will be no classes tomorrow either. You learn from what you see." He went home, dug up his rifle, and as he left town he was heard saying something about a "second round." We were not sure what he meant by that, and we never saw him again.

One of the philanthropic organizations opened a branch in the square and handed out food and clothing to the families of the informers. In other towns, the surviving informers who were to be tried by the courts began to return to their local security stations, saying, "We're here on behalf of the Allies."

Allied commissions in the capital founded new military courts, even before founding our new military. The courts were to try Mountain Fighters who had been accused of committing crimes. There were so many demonstrations throughout the country that the Allies gave the surviving informers police uniforms to restore peace and order. Then the Allies appointed a temporary government to soothe passions, as the newspapers wrote, and the government was given generous financial and military aid. There were daily arrivals of experts whom the Allies had commissioned to reorganize the rest of our national institutions and to use their know-how to improve agriculture, fishing, and light industry. By that time, most of the Mountain Fighters had been rounded up and put into detention camps, and the Security Police made files for men and women over twelve years of age. It also made new I.D. cards and began to issue "Certificates of Good Social Standing." Without a certificate, one could not find a job, go to school, own a radio, or vote in local and national elections.

When elections finally took place, even a lot of people who did have certificates refused to vote, saying, "Let the Allies find others to peel their banana." After the elections, the temporary government became permanent, which the Allies said was a great victory for freedom and democracy, since the security of our country was again threatened by anarchist elements from within, and by imperialist appetites from without. We heard this on Aunt Anna's radio, which was still unlicensed, since she did not qualify for a Certificate of Good Social Standing.

XXIX

When Ermina came out of the hospital with her last bullet wound healed, she and Uncle Iasson moved together into one of the abandoned houses near Grandfather's. They rebuilt the roof, got new doors and windows, painted inside and out, repaired the floors, leveled and planted the yard. When the priest found out about it, he spoke out in the church, calling them sinners and adulterers. He then advised the people to evict Uncle Iasson and Ermina, but the elders were skeptical. They talked about it briefly, then dropped the subject, saying, "There are other more important matters to worry about in our town." The new police chief was furious at everybody. "Now, this is a fine example of anarchy," he said, and warned my uncle that if he and Ermina refused to legitimize their relationship, Ermina would be arrested on prostitution charges.

No one knew exactly why Uncle Iasson and Ermina didn't want to be married, since they already lived like a family. It was an unusual arrangement, but not the only one around. A lot of things like that had happened in the past few years. They were part of the war, or so it seemed, but when the war came to an end, we were still familiar with them.

LOVE
AND
MARRIAGE

Although people would often say, "Isn't this a strange situation?" they were not necessarily offended by it. But the priest said, "Your tolerance toward adultery is proof of your own sinfulness. . . . And if you don't take action, the authority will, Amen."

When Uncle Iasson told Ermina about it, she began to cry, and the neighborhood women gathered to give her advice.

"Don't be stubborn, my daughter," said an old woman. "Think about getting married not because that goat the priest or the police say so, but because of your own happiness and of the children you might soon have."

"If there is love, you can do without the wedding," said another woman. "On the other hand, a wedding ceremony can't destroy the love, can it?"

"Do it, if only to shut their mouths, and to protect yourself from their hypocrisy," advised another. "And to spite the old goat, you can always choose another priest, and have the wedding in a countryside chapel."

Ermina was thinking about it. "I don't want it, but I guess we have no choice," she said at the end. And when the women left, she was still crying.

A
DREAM
COME
TRUE

Uncle Iasson and Ermina planned to take a trip to the capital to do some shopping for the wedding. The night before the trip, Ermina had a dream from which she woke up crying. She went to see the old woman across the street.

"Don't take this trip, my daughter," said the old woman after Ermina had related the dream to her. "After all, how are you going to buy anything without money?"

Ermina was thoughtful. "First, we are going to do a bit of window-shopping, then we'll see," she said.

The old woman shook her head sadly, but maybe

that was later, when my uncle and Ermina came back from shopping. "Go on, tell me the dream one more time, my daughter," she said.

"Well, when we got to the capital, I saw a beautiful gown in a window, and the shopkeeper invited me to try it on. 'May I ask how much it is?' I asked. 'For you, almost nothing,' he said. 'You can have this expensive gown for only one hair, one long gold hair from your head.' Isn't that the strangest thing? We thought he was teasing us, but he insisted he was serious, so I pulled out one of my hairs and gave it to him. What could I lose? It was like a dream coming true."

"And then?"

"Then we stopped at a jeweler's. 'How much for the wedding bands?' 'No gold can match the gold of your hair,' he said, 'so I'll let you have both bands for only one of your hairs.' 'And these earrings?' 'Aquamarine,' he explained. 'Two for one.' I gave him two hairs, but he took only one of them—one for both earrings. 'And the bracelet?' 'Same price,' he said. We bought two bracelets and a necklace. The price always the same."

"And then? What happened then?" asked the old woman.

"We went to the shoe store and to other shops for clothing, furniture, utensils, appliances. My hair began to thin out, and Iasson—poor Iasson!—kept saying, 'That's enough. Let's go back now.' But how could I? We needed so many things for our home, for him, for myself. Hairs grow back, I thought, but an opportunity like this doesn't come along every day. Iasson, poor Iasson, didn't say another word. I went on. I went on buying, and before the end of the day all my hair was gone. My hair, my beautiful hair will not grow back anymore."

The old woman from across the street shook her head again sadly, but maybe that was several weeks after Uncle Iasson and Ermina had been married.

PYRRHA One morning Uncle Iasson woke up and Ermina was not there. He went out looking for her, but he didn't find her anywhere. No one had heard a thing about where she might be. Uncle Iasson began to take trips to other towns in hopes of finding his wife, and Grandfather worried about him because each new trip that my uncle took was longer than the one before, and each time he came back he looked pale, wrinkled, and older. Then he too disappeared. He took a long trip and never came back.

Whenever a traveler passed by, Grandfather and I stopped him and asked if he'd seen my uncle, or heard about him. Only one of them had something to say to us, and that had mostly to do with Ermina. She had been seen in an island sanctuary, younger, much younger than we knew her, and she had changed her name to Pyrrha. "A sanctuary all her own," said the traveler, "and a tall tree for the slow hours of noon." Each noon, she returned from the ocean with another young man, and the school-children wondered whether or not she ever loved the same man for more than a day. "When the sun goes down, she climbs down the tree alone, and the sea rises to meet her toes," said the traveler. And he said, "On her naked body there are imprints of leaves and minnows. Old lovers of hers loiter by the door of her sanctuary, growing older," he said. And he said, "That's where some women find their frustrated husbands, while other women arrive to praise her, and the priest of the island stops by to bless her with rosewater and rosemary."

XXX

In the middle of the town square, the government
erected an obelisk on which the names of the fallen
informers were engraved in gold, and on Indepen-
dence Day the Veterans of Legitimate Wars and
the schoolchildren, led by their new teacher, pa-
raded and placed wreaths of laurel at the base of
the monument.

Although education on the elementary level was
compulsory, Philippos, Flisvos, and I did not have
to go back to school when the government sent a
new teacher that autumn. All of us who had become twelve years old were given a grammar school
diploma, and were expected to apply for Certificates of Good Social Standing, or leave.

Aunt Anna had already been arrested for operat-
ing an unlicensed radio, and Aris was taken away a
day before his wedding.

The radio stopped broadcasting military music,
and began to play love songs in translation. There
were new informers strolling around the square, or
playing cards in the cafés most of the day. And
people kept saying to one another, "Be silent." Or,
"Dip your tongue in your brain before you say a

TWELVE

word—these are difficult times." They now agreed that the newspapers were a bunch of lies, but they read the papers every day and tried to explain the lies to each other. They lived their lives passively, as if something irreplaceable had been taken from them, but if one asked them, they couldn't name it. They just shrugged, saying, "We've seen worse."

Philippos, Flisvos, and I saw them for the last time that Sunday afternoon on the Promontory, where they'd gathered to peer at the horizon, for hours on end, silently, to see if the ship was coming, and if its sail were white or black. We watched them standing there, dark against the autumn light, waiting, waiting until dusk. No ship with either white or black sail showed on the horizon, and everyone shook his head, or murmured to himself, "Maybe tomorrow, maybe the day after . . ."

"The ship will never be back in these waters," said Philippos.

"What are we going to do? How are we going to get out of here?" said Flisvos, rubbing his good eye with the back of his hand. He was crying.

"The other kids have agreed to gather in the fields late tonight," said Philippos.

"Where in the fields?"

"At the Crossroads. I think they'll take off from there," said Philippos.

"I'd go," said Flisvos.

"I'd go too," said Philippos.

"So would I."

We decided to go to bed early.

THE
LAST
TREE
SINGS

I went to Grandfather's to help prepare a supper of fried fish and salad. Grandfather was resting in a long chair next to the pomegranate tree. I spread the tablecloth on the ground, and brought out a carafe of wine. It was still dusk. There were clouds and a reverberation of thunder. The cool autumn breeze crept over the bare soil, wrinkling the surface of the wine in our glasses, and then it blew through the foliage of the small tree and stroked Grandfather's hair. Grandfather closed his eyes, smiling. He was pleased. The pomegranate tree began to sing.

A crack of lightning tore its way down, striking a distant hilltop. A column of water sprang up from the top of the hill, and it kept rising until it reached the clouds. Soon, another bolt of lightning hit the town square, and again the water leapt to the sky. A third one fell even closer, releasing a spring of water right on our street. I was scared. I ran for shelter into the kitchen. I stood behind the kitchen window, shaking. The next flash of lightning could easily find its way to me through that window. I rushed to the bedroom, the windows of which were always shut during the day, but then I remembered Grandfather, and I ran out into the garden again.

As I helped him up, lightning struck the pomegranate tree, setting it aflame. We hurried to the bedroom. In the dark, I heard the soft sound of breathing. I walked in on tiptoe. When I approached the double bed, I saw my father and Uncle Iasson sleeping in it side by side. Slowly, Grandfather climbed into bed and lay down between his two sons, falling asleep right away.

"This land, a narrow strip between rocks and seas, can afford only so many of us. It has no trees, no water—only an illusion of trees and water," Grandfather said. "Even when our crops and livestock were not being taken away, nor our springs filled with corpses and muck, a dozen or so young men and women of your age would gather once a year, first on the Promontory, then in the bay to wait for

ONLY
SO
MANY

217

the ship, while parents and other relatives consoled themselves by saying, 'They'll make a fortune in exile, and they'll come back one day.' No one ever returned. The ship came back empty, came back for more," Grandfather said. "This land can afford only so many of us; the rest will have to go. . . . One way or another," he said.

CODA   Mother had gone to bed and fallen asleep with a black scarf over her face. I got up and clipped my hair and dressed, and when I looked at her again I saw two wet darker patches where the scarf covered her eyes. I opened the window and climbed down quietly, being careful not to wake the neighborhood dogs, and walked out of town toward the fields, shuddering at the sound of bats on the wing and the luminous stare of the owl.

ABOUT THE AUTHOR

Stratis Haviaras was born in the town of Néa Kíos, in Greece, in 1935. He worked for many years in the construction trades. Four books of his poems appeared in Athens between 1963 and 1972. Mr. Haviaras came to the United States in 1967 and has since worked in the Harvard University Library, where he is currently the Curator of the poetry collections. For several years he edited *Arion's Dolphin*, a quarterly of poetry. He began to write in English six years ago, and in 1976 Cleveland State University published a book of his new poems, *Crossing the River Twice*. Most recently he has edited *The Poet's Voice*, a collection on tape of readings by major American poets, published by Harvard University Press. *When the Tree Sings* is his first novel.